Spiral of Silence

Elvira Sánchez–Blake

Spiral
of
Silence

A Novel

Translated from the Spanish by Lorena Terando
Foreword by Debra A. Castillo

 CURBSTONE BOOKS / NORTHWESTERN UNIVERSITY PRESS
EVANSTON, ILLINOIS

Curbstone Books
Northwestern University Press
www.nupress.northwestern.edu

English translation copyright © 2019 by Lorena Terando. Published 2019 by
Curbstone Books / Northwestern University Press. Originally published in 2009 as
Espiral de silencios, copyright © Elvira Sánchez-Blake. All rights reserved.

Printed in the United States of America

10 9 8 7 6 5 4 3 2 1

Library of Congress Cataloging-in-Publication Data
Names: Sánchez-Blake, Elvira E. (Elvira Elizabeth), author. | Terando, Lorena,
    translator.
Title: Spiral of silence : a novel / Elvira Sánchez-Blake ; translated from the Spanish
    by Lorena Terando ; foreword by Debra A. Castillo.
Other titles: Espiral de silencios. English
Description: Evanston : Curbstone Books / Northwestern University Press, 2019.
Identifiers: LCCN 2018034825| ISBN 9780810139169 (pbk. : alk. paper) | ISBN
    9780810139176 (ebook)
Classification: LCC PQ8180.429.A478 .E7713 2019 | DDC 863.7—dc23
LC record available at https://lccn.loc.gov/2018034825

To my Angels

Roberto and Victoria

Peace will not be drowned out by the spiral of silence.

—SANTIAGO CORONADO, "RECUERDOS DE ELSA ALVARADO,"

EL TIEMPO, MAY 25, 1997

CONTENTS

Debra A. Castillo

In the late 1990s, Elvira Sánchez-Blake, just returned from a research trip to Colombia, stopped by my office to fill me in on her extraordinary conversations with women in *la militancia*, which she was beginning to mull over for her dissertation project. She also showed me a photograph of a powerful weaving that she had discovered in a shop in Bogotá but that—alas!—she was unable to purchase on her budget as a graduate student. She went back to the store again and again, and eventually learned more about the artist who created the piece and her personal brush with the organized violence devastating Colombia during those years. That artist, Inés, became one of the key interlocutors in the testimonial part of her dissertation project, and has continued to haunt Elvira Sánchez-Blake's work to this day.

Those rich conversations, and that weaving, turned up in two projects that Sánchez-Blake was working on in parallel. These were complementary ways of synthesizing and coming to terms with the recent past of her country, and with the way its legacy of violence has profoundly shaped (and deformed) the lives of women and children, who were all too often, and until very recently, inexplicably left out of official versions of that history. In her scholarly book, *Patria se escribe con sangre* (*Homeland Is Written in Blood* [Barcelona: Anthropos, 2000]), Sánchez-Blake describes her encounter this way (in my translation):

> The first time I saw Inés was in her handicraft store, which I visited as a customer. I remember that when I entered the shop my attention was drawn to a loom, or an agave fiber weaving that represented the figure of a woman. I was amazed by the expression, the combination of pain and stoicism that the artist was able to achieve with the crisscrossing strings. The figure's expression was so clear and, at the same time, so ambiguous that I had to find out more about the artist. That was when Inés turned up, and she was both the owner of the establishment and the creator of the work: "It's called 'Woman' and it costs 800,000 pesos ($800)." (19)

The piece turns up again in this novel, *Spiral of Silence*, in a chapter called "The Tapestry," where it becomes the work of Mariate: "This particular piece was two meters long and one meter wide. I looked at it as my masterpiece. The undefined sketch of what appeared to be a woman was beginning to take shape in the middle of the tapestry. Everyone at the San Juan co-op was working hard on at least one piece for the Santafé de Antioquia craft fair. . . . Every tapestry showcased our technical skill, mastery, and art, and each motif carried our message of social community and solidarity."

Elvira Sánchez-Blake's work, both scholarly and creative, takes its cue from this metaphor of the stiff fiber, twisted into artistic form, carrying with its creative expression a message of solidarity and advocacy. Fittingly, the novel's opening offers a first artistic sketch. It gives a complete gloss of the novel in the form of three poems, highlighting three women's perspectives as if the outline of their shape in the tapestry. The novel itself is presented as the work of a fourth character—that artist, who has twisted these voices and threads into shape, and who is only revealed only at the end of the novel. Thus, there is Mariate, the artist and mother of three boys whose lives take on iconic form in Colombia's violent turn-of-the millennium situation; Norma, an upper-class military wife and adoptive mother of one of these sons; and Amparo, the lover of another of them. Along the way, the book highlights their intersections with three other women, warp and weft on the loom of their lives: Carmen, the nanny who mediates between Mariate and Norma; Nora, the guerrillera and (later) UN/Amnesty International representative; and Madre Susana, the reluctant nun, and even more reluctant prison warden. These stories are twisted together in the novel in a series of micro-chapters that continuously change point of view as the threads of their lives interweave, creating a single image of the suffering, powerful woman.

The focus of this narrative is the time period between the early 1980s and the middle of the first decade of this century. Part I culminates on a somber note with the attack on the Palace of Justice by the guerrilla group M-19 on November 6, 1985. This set piece is matched in the second part of the book with a violent battle in the fictional town that had served as Mariate's refuge. The two brutal exchanges intentionally echo each other. As if to underline this, a village elder offers this wisdom to Amparo as young people prepare to murder each other: "I've been watching this same war play out the same way for decades. The only difference is the year. It's like a bad movie they remake every twenty years, swapping out old actors with new ones who are even nastier." As Friedrich Engels wrote to his friend Karl Marx on December 3, 1851 (in a phrase made much more famous in Marx's published version a year later): "It really seems as though old Hegel, in the guise of the World Spirit, were directing history from the grave and, with the greatest conscientiousness, causing everything to be re-enacted twice over, once as grand tragedy and the second time as rotten farce." Parts 1 and 2 of Sánchez-Blake's novel are precisely that: history written and reenacted in the tragedy of the Palace of Justice, the rotten melodrama of the battle in San Juan.

In the Palace of Justice crossfire, approximately 120 people lost their lives, including most of the guerrillas and twelve Supreme Court judges. The second, fictional battle reflects more generally the ongoing violence during that entire twenty-year period. It encapsulates significant trauma. According to the *¡Basta ya!* study published in 2012 by the Centro Nacional de Memoria Histórica (National Center for Historical Memory), 218,094 people died in the conflict between 1958 and 2012, most of them civilians (177,307 civilians and 40,787 fighters). At the same time, 25,007 people disappeared; there were 27,023 kidnappings, and 5,712,506 civilians were forced from their homes. These are significant numbers for any country, and represent a startlingly high percentage of the population of a country whose total number of inhabitants in that period ranged from 30 million to 40 million.

Elvira Sánchez-Blake titled her novel *Spiral of Silence*, and indeed, the portrait of the Colombian woman—whether in agave fiber or in black-and-white words on a page—may seem at first glance to evoke a long history of repression and silence. Nothing could be further from the truth. Like the evocative fiber art piece, Sánchez-Blake's novel reminds us of the urgent voices of contemporary Colombian women in many genres—in their handicraft shops, festival displays, NGOs, public protests, memoirs, testimonios, novels, and plays. These women are breaking the silence and taking leadership in a population that is actively contesting their nation's violent legacy—advocating, in the words of Mexican poet Rosario Castellanos, for another way to be.

TRANSLATOR'S INTRODUCTION

There is a persistent negative connotation attached to being a translator, to writing a translation. The overriding narrative is that it is "less than," there is inevitably "loss," and readers of a translation can never *really* get the picture the author of the source text intended to publish.

Yet a translation that offers access to a text for readers unable to access the source text cannot be "less than." It represents only gain. In any act of communication—monolingual or otherwise—there is always as much potential for gain as there is for loss. And readers of any source text, once it ventures from its author's keyboard or pen or pencil stroke, are free to interpret the picture the author paints in a way that is at the very least tinged by their own experiences and understandings. So it is with translation. Translation is one more form of the complicated system of communication that language offers, and we translators are crucial players in that communication.

My strategy in translating this work reflects that. I strove to create a text that flows well in English, while at the same time showcasing its undeniable Colombianness. Throughout the text readers find words in Spanish that are easily recognizable in English, even to someone who hasn't studied Spanish ("guerrilla," or "comandante," for example), and other words in Spanish that are less ubiquitous in Anglo culture and therefore call readers' attention to the origin of the text (such as "arepa de choclo," a typically Colombian corn cake; or "don" and "doña," honorifics that that imply deep respect). When the Spanish word is less recognizable, its meaning is incorporated into the body of the text. When there are references to historical events and/or proper names, readers may find a definition and contextualization in the glossary at the end of the book.

So the design of the translation was to flow well in English and to showcase Colombia. That I chose this particular book to translate speaks to my will to add women's voices to the literary conversation about the impact of the war in Colombia. And to my will to offer a view of Colombia that relies less on what we always hear about it—the drug trade, coffee, paramilitaries, and guerrilla groups—and more on its complexities, through the perspectives of four women, their experiences, and their memories of their experiences.

Many people have contributed to my translator's "black box," and I am deeply grateful to them. Guillermo Cohen was a constant resource and steadfast supporter through the many years it took to bring this translation to light. Jonathan Tittler, professor emeritus of Hispanic studies (Rutgers University) and an accomplished translator, has provided invaluable insights, corrections, and suggestions. The author, Elvira Sánchez Blake, was always available to provide clarification and to read and reread drafts to ensure accuracy. And others, perhaps less knowingly, got me out of many a terminological tight spot: Andrew Porter, John Terando III, Denise Aughenbaugh, and Jessica Banks, in particular. A thank-you is hardly enough. But I thank them nonetheless.

Spiral of Silence

María Teresa

I gave him his life, and I took it away.
Does absolution come only by sacrifice?
Where's the oracle that this sentence foretold?
The command to sacrifice my flesh and blood?
I gave him his life, and I condemned him, too.
Before the court of man I plead innocent.
Before the court of the gods I plead guilty.
Before the court of history I plead victim.
And you, I pronounce you judges.
I beg for your mercy.

Norma

I stole him. I was punished.
I fancied myself redeemer but was myself redeemed.
The mark of Cain blazoned on his forehead cast gloom over his life.
We're both victim and victimizer in a tragedy
repeated century after century.
Now I can tell my story
so that you will not be from the outset caught unawares.

Amparo

I am the crossroads
where paths intersect.
I was the keeper of the prophecy,
the offering required by the gods.
I was witness, seer, and heroine,
lover, confidante, and storyteller.
The key to the enigma is unveiled right before our eyes
through this story that converges in
the fates of brother against brother in a ruthless war,
strewing the streets with innocents in
a never-ending spiral of silence.

Part One

Comandante

Amparo

Anyone who knows him says he walks into a room and takes command. He's tall but not towering, striking with his curly hair and muscular build. A man of few words, he is firm but fair. He must have been an army officer at one time, because he is good at balancing authority and compassion. His military training and refined Jesuit schooling were clearly ingrained in him. Comandante is young, but nonetheless his ranks obey him without question. He always has good advice for his subordinates—and his superiors—at the tip of his tongue. He cannot abide disobedience, lack of discipline, or lack of responsibility. He doesn't drink and doesn't seem to have any vices. No one has ever heard him talk about a wife, children, or personal drama. But they do know that Comandante declared all-out war on the guerrilla to avenge his family. The army wouldn't give him what he needed to do away with his enemies, so he joined Carlos Castaño's paramilitary group, and he trained and he trained. He was wholly dedicated to eliminating the guerrilla through "social cleansing."

Comandante and his squad of lieutenants had been hanging around since Monday, according to the village shopkeeper don Eusebio, scoping out the town square and all around it. The village teacher doña Marina said they were stopping the kids and asking questions. And the gossip from Banco Agrario was that on Tuesday, Comandante deposited a hefty chunk of change in the account of some guy named Fidel. The villagers don't trust them. If they happen to cross paths, folks pick up their pace, or hide behind their shawls, or under their hats. Some are even packing their bags to hightail it out before they start threatening people.

Because once the threats start, there's no going back. First, they start pointing fingers at people, then they start pushing them around until, finally, they select their scapegoats. The next step is to kick out the authorities, anyone with any influence, until they've taken over the entire village and become its owners, the *señores*. Hope is not an option. There is no compassion. Their mission is to exterminate. They call it "counter-insurgency."

It is no secret. The paramilitaries work with narco-traffickers because the narcos fund them; the paras protect the narcos and rake in profits, living rich—and cruel and intimidating. Everyone knows the war has many sides, but in the end, it comes down to a simple fight over the best land for drug crops.

I was the only one who wasn't scared by their being there. I saw them walk over to the juice stand on San Juan plaza that Friday, and I did what I always do when someone new comes to this podunk town. Confident and provocative, I strolled over to take their order.

"What can I get you?" I purred.

His buddies ordered *lulo* or tamarind juice right away, but Comandante took his time, looking me up and down before he answered.

"Passion fruit, *por favor*."

I didn't even bat an eye—I knew what I had and wasn't ashamed to flaunt it—and flashed him one of my best smiles. His response was to stare at me, curious. He took off his sunglasses so his eyes could focus. I took advantage to check out the color of his eyes.

"Not bad, not bad at all," I said to myself.

My mom made their drinks and laid down a stern warning: "Be careful with those guys, Amparo. They aren't from around here. Who knows what they have up their sleeves!"

A Baby in Prison
Mariate

Miguel's birth was an extraordinary occasion at Medellín's Buen Pastor prison. Inmates and guards alike flooded into the prison's sickbay as the midwives helped me give birth. My friends, the *compañeras* with the most mamá experience, fought over who was going to coach me in breastfeeding, or teach me how to change his diapers and clean his belly button. Others argued about who was going to lay the aloe leaves on me for the baby's future happiness. They even did a cleansing to purge our jail cells of evil spirits. My compañeras had crocheted little booties and bonnets, rompers and receiving blankets for the baby. It ended up a big fiesta with quite a bit of commotion until Madre Superiora appeared and commanded silence.

"What are you going to name him?" she demanded.

"Miguel Angel," I said.

"Is that the father's name?"

"No, it's for the archangel Miguel, the invincible," was my reply.

But she wasn't paying any attention to me; she was busy with the birth certificate.

When I was finally alone with my little baby boy, I cradled him in my arms. He was so fragile, it took my breath away. I was barely fifteen, but I knew I was ready to raise him. My family had disowned me the second I landed in jail, and my boyfriend was in jail, too. But I didn't care. I'd get by with the help of my compañeras. I swore I would, again and again.

◎

Mariate had come to the Buen Pastor of an afternoon six months before, and Nora—a self-assured, all-around good person—was the only one who had welcomed her.

"So, what did you do to land in here, baby girl, *sardina?*

When Mariate explained why she was there, Nora hugged her and started shouting: "You're one of us, comrade!"

"But I'm not a revolutionary! I didn't do it! It really is all a big misunderstanding."

Mariate told her what had happened. Early one morning an army patrol burst through the door. Bellowing and shouting obscenities, they razed the place and destroyed what little there was. When Mariate saw the weapons they pulled out from the bottom of a trunk, she barely had the time to question Julián with her eyes before he was gone. They dragged him out in cuffs to an army truck, and that was all she knew. She was taken to Buen Pastor. She was surprised by what they were charging her with: subversion, possession of weapons, conspiracy against the state, and a long string of incomprehensible crimes. She had no defense or argument. Nora's reaction to her story surprised Mariate. Nora listened closely; then, as Mariate finished, she looked at her for a bit and told her she should take responsibility for her part in the weapons theft.

"You're a revolutionary. It will be a lot easier for you if you take up the people's cause head-on instead of denying it."

When she saw Mariate's belly she got even more excited. "Plus, just think of the responsibility you have; you will be the mother of a child of the revolution! We are your compañeras, and we'll help you out."

Nora was a true-blue *paisa* from Antioquia; she was confident, comical, and plucky. She got it into her head to take up a collection among the compañeras in cell block eight, where political prisoners were held, and she led a campaign so they would let Mariate keep her baby in prison. They were all betting on baby names. Some were saying she should call her little one "Libertad," for liberty. No, "Victoria," for victory; or "Esperanza," for hope! But Mariate was emphatic: The baby will be a boy, and he'll be named after an archangel. The money collected allowed her to get a crib, some clothes, diapers, and even a basket full of Johnson & Johnson baby products.

◎

It was because of my friendship with Nora that I didn't have more problems than I already did. Honestly, I felt very welcomed. It wasn't long before I had become politically engaged and joined the ELN, the Ejército de Liberación Nacional (National Liberation Army). That was how I came to read revolutionary treatises. I learned slogans and began to use sophisticated political terminology. We weren't "friends" anymore; we were "compañeras," "comrades." The "class struggle" would put an end to differences and hierarchies, and the cost of living was called "surplus value." My revolutionary conscience was awakened through secret debates over the legacy of Camilo Torres and the ELN's newsletter *NUPALOM*, "*Ni un paso atrás liberación o muerte*," or "Not one step back, freedom or death." In short order, I felt part of the rhetoric that, although it was a bit foreign for me, nonetheless granted me entry into what seemed to be the prison's most respected group. I convinced myself that my boyfriend had done something honorable when he'd stored the ELN's weapons, and that my sentence was justified for the sake of the struggle for and by the people. In the end, I was sentenced to seven years with no trial or appeal. I wasn't even granted early release for pregnancy because I was a political prisoner. But at least they let me keep the baby in prison.

When Miguel was born, I was given a crib to set up in my cell, and my compañeras set up a schedule to help me take care of him. One nun felt sorry for me and taught me to knit. I loved it from the start. Soon my hands were creating itty-bitty sweaters and caps, and tiny, brightly colored ruanas, ponchos that were just adorable on my little man. The first six months went by with me juggling the baby, knitting, and revolutionary slogans. Miguel grew healthy and strong. Little by little he turned into the perfect accomplice for secret meetings, or smuggling love letters in his diapers and bottles. He was the balm for the mamás whose kids weren't with them; he was the longing of young nuns; and the reason for living of disenchanted prostitutes. He was joy in a place where we were all surrounded by hardship and festering, shattered dreams.

The Hole
Mariate

Everything fell apart when the M-19, the Movimiento 19 de abril (April 19th Movement), guerrilla commando took over the embassy of the Dominican Republic in Bogotá. They took hostage more than thirty diplomats from the United States, Venezuela, Brazil, Austria, Costa Rica, Haiti, the Dominican Republic, Switzerland, Guatemala, Uruguay, Mexico, Israel, Egypt, and even the Vatican's Apostolic nuncio. The operation was called "Democracy and Freedom," and the M-19 compañeros were using it to denounce human rights violations by the military, to draw attention to the penal justice system (aka torture chambers), and to negotiate freedom for the political prisoners packing the country's prisons.

The inmates heard about it at lunch. The TV program was interrupted suddenly by live footage of a barrage of gunfire as the guerrilleros in soccer sweats took over the embassy. Mariate was nursing the baby when Nora and the "Progreso" group started to cheer for the M-19. The magnitude of the event fanned the flames of revolutionary fervor as the rebels called for freedom for all political prisoners. The very thought sent all the political prisoners into a frenzy of excitement. They felt the prison doors swinging open before them, and started banging on tables and chairs, shouting: "Freedom! Freedom! Freedom!" Their joy turned to rage, and things started to get out of control. Common criminals joined in the fray, but on the other side. They hated the proud politicals because they had the advantage of the strength of the revolution, and the spat ballooned into physical confrontations, fistfights, and attacks. Cell block five showed up with knives and started stabbing the compañeras, and then all hell broke loose. Madre Superiora tried in vain to tamp down the riot. She had to call the military police, and a battalion rushed in with tear gas.

13

We all ended up in the Hole. There was no mercy. The Hole was a dark, somber dungeon for insubordinates. We were there for a week in isolation, broken in body and in spirit, wallowing in the squalor of our own excrement and menstrual blood mingled with scraps of food the nuns tossed at us like wild dogs. Our only comfort was to shout at the top of our lungs and curse our captors. We had no idea what had happened with the takeover or with M-19's plans to negotiate the release of political prisoners. And it was even worse for me. I was completely cut off from my baby that whole time. I cried so much, both my milk and my tears went dry. The guards turned a deaf ear to my pleas. It made them happy to see me so desperate. All I wanted was information about my baby: Who was taking care of him? Where was he? I was petrified they were going to let him starve to death on me. He had been breastfed exclusively till then.

After a week, they let us out. My legs could hardly hold me up, I was so weak. It took me a while to adjust to the light again, and I'd had so little food that waves of dizziness would overtake me. We soon found out that the embassy takeover was not over and no end was in sight. The M-19 and the hostages seemed to have found a rhythm amid the negotiations between the guerrillas' delegate Chiqui and a government commission. Reporters had set up a camp called Villa Chiva near the Dominican embassy, and their reports made it look like the M-19 was having a grand old time over there with their hostages, while we almost died in here for supporting them.

I was taken straight to Madre Superiora. I was unsteady on my feet, pretty dizzy, and she was stern . . . Right then and there, she informed me that my baby had been placed with a foster family for the duration of my sentence.

"What? You can't do that!" I shouted as my world came crashing down around me.

"We have been breaking prison rules by letting the minor stay here as long as he did. Military authorities find it highly undesirable for a child to be raised under these conditions. They punished me for having allowed it, and I had to make a drastic decision. This is no place to raise a child, and he will be much better off with a family."

I pleaded and begged, but it did no good. The nun was stoic. She had a heart of stone. She said I might be able to see him on visiting days and assured me that of course I would get my baby back as soon as my sentence was up.

"I'm in for seven years! When I get out my son won't even recognize me," I countered.

"That is not my problem. You are not in a position to take care of him, and I cannot take care of an infant in a penitentiary. Didn't you see what happened? If you are incapable of maintaining good behavior and following prison regulations, you can't be responsible for your son, either. If it makes you feel any better, I can assure you that the boy is being raised in better conditions than you could hope to offer him. The family taking care of him treats him very, very well. As if he were their equal."

As if he were their equal? This was even worse than the Hole. I could not hold back the nausea, and I retched and retched until what little there was in my stomach was emptied. I screamed, I begged, I swore. None of it made a bit of difference.

The nun was disgusted and sent me from her office, threatening me with another week in the Hole if I didn't stop hounding her.

On the way back to my cell, I ran into Nora and collapsed into her arms.

"Nora, let's get out of here. The M-19 is going to get us out, right? I have to get my son back." She was my only hope; she always had a solution for everything. Except now. My paisa friend was firm and pulled my feet straight back down to earth.

"Sardina, come down out of the clouds. Political prisoners are not going to be let out. The military will never let that happen."

Then Nora told me what I didn't yet know. She related the details of how she was ambushed with an ELN commando and subsequently captured by the military. She had survived three months of horrendous torture in the Caballerizas, the army stables, before she was transferred to Buen Pastor.

After an M-19 commando stole over five thousand weapons from the army's Northern Canton Battalion in Bogotá, the military had been gripped by a relentless need to punish any and all who had even the slightest connection to revolutionaries. This was when the big guns from M-19 and quite a few other groups all fell. The government gave the army carte blanche to carry out counter-revolutionary operations, with no regard for details like human rights. It was Defense Minister Camacho Leyva's term, complete with torture chambers. No one was spared the techniques they refined there. Repression had shot up, which explained why prisons were bursting at the seams with political prisoners, and why so many innocent people who had nothing to do with it had been caught up in it all.

My thoughts turned to Julián. I hadn't heard anything from him in so long. Was he alive or dead? He, too, had ended up in the army's Caballerizas.

"Don't get your hopes up, *amiga*," Nora warned me. "Most don't make it out alive. If I were you, I would be praying for your Julián's soul."

But I didn't know whether to pray for his soul or curse it. My sentence had not been too brutal so far because I had my baby with me. But now I was beginning to realize the extent of my punishment. I knew I had lost my little Miguel forever. Julián was probably dead, and on top of that, my family had cut me off. As the days passed, I slid further and further into the depths of depression. I spent my time watching shadows dance on the cement walls of my cell, thinking that if I let myself go, my mind would plunge into the darkness as the last little remnants of light faded through the chinks in the walls.

A Prisoner's Baby

Norma

When my husband came home holding a baby in his arms that he said was a prisoner's, I was overwhelmed by misgivings.

"And doesn't he have a family, a father, or someone to take care of him?"

"No one is stepping forward," he responded matter-of-factly. "The mother can't take care of him in prison, and odds are she won't want him when she gets out. You know that kind of people; they pop out kids but have not one iota of responsibility."

I contemplated the little bundle wrapped up in a yellow poncho, while Ricardo tried to calm him down. He was wailing incessantly. I came closer, examined him, and took him in my arms, trying hard to tamp down the nausea welling up inside me. I held him close, and the little guy calmed down for a moment, looking at me curiously. Clearly, he was neglected, but he was healthy, and I was quickly and hopelessly captivated by his adorable hazel eyes.

◎

Ricardo and Norma Restrepo lived in the El Poblado gated community. Ricardo was a colonel in the army so they could have lived on base in officers' housing, but they chose to live in the housing complex because it was more family-oriented. Actually, the colonel would have preferred to live on base, but he had agreed to Norma's request so as to score some points with her and her family. Norma was thirty-five, and she considered herself fortunate in her life with all its comforts. The only thing that was hard on her was the fact that she couldn't have children. They had thought about adopting but had put it on hold while they waited for a miracle. It wasn't so much that she needed to have a baby, as how irritated she was at being left out every time she got together

17

with friends, and the conversation turned to the ups and downs of raising kids, challenging teenagers, and the gazillion satisfactions of motherhood.

⊚

"Do you think we could adopt him?" I ventured.

"Legally, his mother is still in the picture, but who knows? Maybe with time we will get attached to him and we'll want to start the adoption process. We'll see," said Ricardo.

"We'll see? And what do you expect us to do if she gets out of prison and comes for him and he has already grown up with us? Or are you saying we should be Good Samaritans, with the kind of person she is? *Dios mío*, Ricardo! My Lord! The things that occur to you! And how can I be sure that this baby isn't . . . well, that he doesn't have some sort of problem? We don't know anything about him. His mother is in prison. She has to have done something awful. You are aware that runs in families, right? I've heard that things like that are genetic."

"She was convicted of subversion."

"Oh, so she's a guerrillera? Even worse! Those people are awful, the worst kind. They are capable of anything! Just look at how they have the whole country in their grip with the embassy takeover. How horrible! What an international embarrassment!"

My husband went silent. I knew he was less concerned about the international embarrassment than he was about the fact that the armed forces had been humiliated.

But Ricardo had one last reason why we should take the baby in.

"My sister asked me if we could take care of the baby for a while."

"And why should we?"

"She is the only family I have. If we don't, he will go to the family welfare foster system in the Instituto Bienestar Familiar. But . . ."

"But what?"

"It would be like a death sentence to leave him in the hands of the state. Think about it. His mother is barely sixteen. What kind of life is this little *muchacho* going to have? Just look what shape he's in now. Prison life is the only life he's known."

Madre Susana was Madre Superiora at Medellín's Buen Pastor prison, and she'd asked him to raise the baby. Ricardo loved his sister and admired her. What in the world were we getting ourselves into? Slowly compassion was starting to win out over suspicion. Of course, I wanted to have a baby, but not

18

like this! Fed from the breast of who knows what kind of woman. A convict! My husband went on.

"He's been in the prison with his mother since he was born, but now they're having problems. The prisoners rioted last week, and the baby was almost killed in the chaos. Those people are half wild. My sister doesn't know what to do. There are no clear national prison management or Ministry of Justice regulations for something like this. It is very rare for inmates to be able to keep their babies while they are serving out their sentences. They made an exception this time because the mother is a minor and she could qualify for the early release for pregnancy program. Oh, and her family disowned her after they found out about her subversive activities."

But it wasn't until his final argument that he won me over.

"If you two form a bond, I will figure out how to get custody."

The baby was getting tired of resisting and finally let me cradle him in my arms. I couldn't help but feel just a hint of tenderness stealing up on me as I watched him fight between sleep and tears. My maternal instinct told me to hold him close to my chest and slowly rock him to sleep. Then I cleaned off his snotty face with a handkerchief and asked: "What's his name?"

"I have it here on this paper. Miguel Angel."

I sent someone to fetch my housekeeper Carmen, whom I trusted implicitly. I instructed her to get rid of the dirty, smelly ruana the baby had come swaddled in. I sent our driver to the El Exito superstore for a complete trousseau of baby clothes, bottles, a crib, a stroller, and other things we'd need. And I laid out my conditions right then and there.

No way would I foster this baby temporarily. Absolutely not! How would I explain to my friends and family that I was fostering an inmate's baby? Not an option. Carmen became his full-time nanny, and I hired a nurse who came a few days a week. The first thing I had to do was make sure the baby was healthy, physically and mentally. The doctors assured me that he was healthy. He was a bit undernourished because God knows how he had been taken care of in the prison, but little by little, with our dedication, he improved. I didn't get my hands dirty, though. I didn't want to be too involved. That was why I had Carmen—she oversaw everything. That woman should feel so thankful that we have taken her baby in, despite his horrible beginnings. Imagine, going from prison to a home with all the comforts, growing up like a decent human being.

◎

It wasn't long before Miguel was part of the circle of muchachos playing on the Los Guaduales complex playground. The Restrepos showed him off like a trophy on the weekends, in fine restaurants and at the military club. He started putting on some baby fat, and soon all the high-society Antioquian ladies were fawning over the handsome little one.

Time passed, and things fell into place. Ricardo and Norma grew accustomed to his presence, and Miguel settled into the blissful life of a spoiled child. At first Carmen was rigid, almost robotic, in her role as nanny. But as she got to know him, her rigidity turned into tenderness. Even Ricardo developed affection for the boy and started spending more time at home. This was the time, Norma came to think, that they were closest to being a happy family.

The San Juan Fiesta

Amparo

I saw him again when I was serving up *limonadas* at the stand on San Juan Plaza. I shot him a look intended to melt the toughest of men. I knew I had him by the smile he flashed back at me as he stood in don Eusebio's shop talking to other men in uniform. When I had served the limonadas, I went over to the shop.

"I'm out of sugar, don Eusebio. Can you spot me a bag, and I'll pay you when my mom gets here?"

I could tell he was watching me from the table in the corner. I motioned to don Eusebio and he shook his head. Then I said out loud: "I suppose you're going to the fiesta with your family tonight?"

"Oh, of course, Amparito! I never miss it! My wife has been primping and preening at the beauty parlor since three."

San Juan was celebrating the fiesta of its patron saint. People streamed in from all around, dressed up and wearing fancy costume jewelry, carrying decorated banners from the church to the square or holding up flower-covered floats, to join in the parades, carnivals, and celebrations. Streets were blocked off so the villagers could mingle and enjoy the music and hubbub, half drunk from the mingled aromas of lily and lemon blossom, *aguardiente* rum, beer, and sweat.

Music thrummed through the plaza speakers across the village, calling everyone to the dance at the community center that night. A rumor got out that there was a *papayera* band coming from Urabá, and the rumor did what rumor should do. People from all across the region started pouring into the plaza that afternoon, milling around the entrance, waiting for tickets to the big bash: the San Juan *parranda*. Folks were belting out the traditional *joropo* chorus, "San Juan, San Juan, San Juan," from the shops and *chicharrería* snack stands.

21

By nightfall the fiesta was bursting with people; it was hot, and the hall was steaming with the sweat of people tapping their feet to the beat of the music on the tile floors. Popular vallenato songs reverberated in every corner of the tiny village. The dancers' sexy outfits clung to their bodies, and they weren't in the least self-conscious as they swiveled their hips seductively and twirled the vallenato or salsa across the dance floor.

Early on a boy from the village pulled me onto the dance floor. I had seen him from time to time, as I had so many others from the area, but this was the first time we had danced together, and I had a chance to get a good look at him. I was captivated by his mischievous smile and the way he moved. We joked and flirted, and soon began to get to know one another. It wasn't long before he was holding me closer and wrapping me in his arms. I was seduced by his humor and warmth. He said his nickname was Mono, even though he was clearly not blond or even light-haired.

I knew I stood out from the girls at the fiesta with my tight hip-huggers and a sexy criss-cross, midriff blouse that accentuated my breasts. I could tell both villagers and newcomers were admiring me. Mono wrapped me in his arms, and I spotted someone at the bar. It was that guy I had seen at don Eusebio's that afternoon, except now he was in civilian clothes. I could feel his eyes glued to my body.

The papayera was playing the first few bars of "La gota fría," a Colombian classic about breaking into a cold sweat during an accordion duel—but not Carlos Vives's version. We all still sang along at the top of our lungs, swaying to the melody's alluring, contagious rhythm: *Me lleva él o me lo llevo yo / pa' que se acabe la vaina. / ¡Ay! Morales, a mí no me lleva / porque no me da la gana, / Moralito, a mí no me lleva / porque no me da la gana . . .*

The village señoras sat in big chairs, stomping the floor to the beat of the drums as they followed the events carefully, on the lookout for new gossip. The men, braver for their aguardiente, argued over the upcoming elections, but they still managed to check out the prettiest chicas at the fiesta from the corners of their eyes. The never-ending circle of provincial tradition was complete.

The song ended and, with it, my captivation. I headed back toward the table where my friends were. I watched my dance partner, who went to sit with a group of chicos at the other end of the room. I was struck by their sallow, stubbly, sun-stained faces; they all wore mountain boots. But Mono was different; he looked terrific with his freshly shaved face and carefully ironed blue jeans and white shirt.

I turned around again, and the guy from the bar was asking me to dance. I didn't hesitate an instant. "I would love to," I said. "La gota fría" gave way to a slower beat.

I felt dizzy, overcome by the heat and the blush of the moment, struck by the come-and-go of the music and the play of the lights flooding the place. A strange power invaded me when I was so close to this man; feelings I'd never had before awakened inside me. *Un mediodía que estuve pensando en la mujer que me hacía soñar*, from "Matilde Lina," played on and on. Having him hold me was heaven for me; we were so close that I was nearly breathing the same breath as this stranger. And I was desperate to uncover the enigma of his undefinable eyes. They weren't brown and they weren't gray. The power of his embrace made me feel faint; yet even with that and the darkness of the place, I could still see a profound loneliness radiating from those eyes. *Llegó de pronto a mi pensamiento esta triste melodía, y como nada tenía, la aproveché en el momento.* Suddenly I was unnerved. I felt like I was being watched. I could see Mono's eyes from the table in the back, fixed on my new dance partner, challenging him. Did they know each other? I started involuntarily as I realized how much they looked alike—as if they were opposites in chiaroscuro. I thought the rivalry between the two was entertaining, but I was also deeply moved by the magnetism that this almost spiritual contact had ignited, like the conjunction of stars converging in the skies. When the song ended, my enigmatic dance partner thanked me kindly, and vanished.

The Letter

Mariate

Crochet stitch, chain stitch, crochet, crochet, chain, crochet. Thread by thread, stitch by stitch, strand by strand, the pattern spread across the skirt, defining the disconnected figures of a piece that had not yet found its form and structure. My mind was an absolute blank as my hands worked tirelessly. The little nun guard sat by my side to crochet on Sundays, while the other inmates welcomed their visitors. We exchanged no words; we just worked our crochet hooks to the measured rhythm of silence superimposed on the emptiness of absence.

But that particular Sunday, I was told I had a visitor. I thought it was odd, since no one had ever visited me. It was Luz Marina, one of Julián's sisters. She brought me a letter that she had managed to sneak through the painstaking security searches at both La Picota prison in Bogotá and the Buen Pastor in Medellín. It was the first time I had heard from him in two and a half years. Stone faced, I put my crocheting aside to read the letter.

> Mariate:
> I heard you had a baby boy in prison. I know it can't be easy, but I have faith that you are strong. This has all been very tough on me, especially the first year. After three months at the Caballerizas they sent me to La Picota. Now I'm doing a little better. When I wanted to give up and just die, I held on tight to the memory of you, and I don't know how, but I made it through. Here I am.

It was probably around the time I lost my baby when Julián found out that I had had him.

25

They say the new administration will grant amnesty to all political prisoners. In here my compañeros and I don't have a whole lot of faith that could happen, but that would be how we could see each other again. I've met very interesting people in here, and I've learned a lot. They lead the M-19 from prison, and they know where they are going. It's done me a lot of good to be on their side, to have their protection. Our prison yard is always buzzing with journalists, politicians, and people who come to interview them and get advice. When I get out, I hope I can join their fight for freedom and justice. This country needs it. I hope you can understand.

Amor, I hope that fate has been kinder to you. After all, you had nothing to do with any of it. What I want most in the world now is to see you again and meet our son.

Julián

Julián. I thought the army had crushed him, but suddenly he had come back to life. He was talking about amnesty. Struggle and social justice? He had clearly gone through the same revolutionary indoctrination I had. The difference was that the only thing I wanted was to get Miguel back. I was elated to hear from Julián, but it was also painful. He didn't even seem to be sorry for getting us into all this mess.

Still, hearing from Julián again was a magical elixir. His letter restored my strength and my will to go on. I would never resign myself to the loss of my son, but I wasn't going to let myself die of a broken heart.

"Amnesty? Ha! Spare me," snorted Nora when she read the letter. "Who's going to fall for the government's hoaxes with its supposed amnesties, cease-fires, and crap!"

"But it's a new administration, and it seems to be clear about what it wants to do. Did you see that the president is paisa?" I countered. Madre Superiora had made sure that all inmates were in the TV room to watch the inauguration. The new president went on and on about dialogue, peace, and solutions for social problems, the purported "objective and subjective causes of subversion." His favorite lines were "not one more drop of blood," and his tired "Sí, se puede!" With the slogans came his promises for social justice. I wasn't really impressed by his political goals, but a possible amnesty renewed my hope that I might get my little Miguel back.

So, I went one last time to Madre Superiora to ask her about my son. She kept saying I should feel so lucky because Miguel was in the care of a family that could give him every imaginable comfort and privilege. She gave me the same old spiel that prison was no place to raise a child, and pointed out once again that they had made an exception for me.

"You must understand that I only want what is best for the boy. A child born and raised in a prison will forever bear the mark of Cain, the stain of a criminal. That is why I took the trouble to place him with a decent family, to save him from that cruel fate. Don't you want what is best for your son, too?"

A decent family? The stain of a criminal? I wasn't convinced by her arguments. My son had done just fine with me and had everything he needed in prison. I feared the worst—that I would never get him back, even when I did get out. And the visits she had promised? Madre Superiora sputtered out some convoluted excuses, effectively postponing that promise indefinitely.

Luz Marina was the only one who worried about them enough to find them both in their respective prisons. And now she was offering Mariate a way to communicate with Julián; she was wondering if Mariate had a letter to send back. But what would she say? How would she explain she'd lost the "baby boy"? And deep down, she blamed Julián for her situation. She said no. No, she didn't have a letter for him. She wanted to be silent for a while longer. For now.

What Julián hadn't told Mariate in his letter was that he had been tortured in the Caballerizas. His left arm was almost useless, and his neck always hurt now. He didn't tell her that nightmares shook him awake at night, sweating and frantic, convinced the guards were coming to submarine him again. They'd hold his head under water and pull it out again, over and over, until he passed out. Then they'd pound his testicles and drag him over gravel until he came to. Then they'd string him up from a branch. One night they left him hanging by his left arm. It popped out of its socket, and now he couldn't move it well. He exercised it and had regained some mobility, but the arm would never be the same.

By the time he was transferred to La Picota, he'd lost so much weight he could barely even stand. The inmates from the M-19 could see immediately he was a political prisoner, and they helped him physically and emotionally. They also trained him for their movement. He met Turco, Afranio, and Almarales in there. They were a powerful front in La Picota; they ran the M-19 from the inside. They even sent out bulletins and press releases from La Picota. Julián

27

wrote some of them: one called *Canas al aire* and one called *El Picotazo*. Those same leaders were also involved in the negotiations when the M-19 took over the embassy of the Dominican Republic. Those days were intense, full of revolutionary fervor. For the entire sixty days that the M-19 held more than forty ambassadors and members of the diplomatic corps, the high command called all the shots from prison. The calls to release political prisoners held for stealing weapons from the Northern Canton were meant for them. The famous Chiqui was the face of the negotiators as mediator, and she earned her country's love by dint of her courage and determination. After two months, as the whole world watched, many of the M-19's conditions were met, including a payment of one million dollars from the government and a commitment to contract a human rights observer. But the prisoners were not freed. Julián witnessed the entire process, and he saw the pain in the prisoners' eyes when they watched on TV as their compañeros boarded a plane to Cuba, to the crowd's standing ovations. The same images were broadcast for the inmates in Buen Pastor, with tight security. It was a political feat—an unprecedented victory for the people who had supported them. But the men in La Picota and the women in Buen Pastor would serve their sentences until further notice.

Amnesty
Norma

Ricardo was in a rage as he walked through the door. Clutched in his hand was a copy of Law 35 of 1982, granting amnesty to political prisoners and giving the president special powers to create a Peace Commission to negotiate with armed groups.

"This is unbelievable!" he roared. "The law frees political suspects and prisoners, ends the state of emergency, and repeals the Security Statute. It even strips the military of its special offices and powers!"

He proceeded to read the president's press release aloud: The country's stakeholders must participate in dialogues and a national referendum, and all political sectors would be fully represented. The Commission for National Dialogue would include representatives from the government, the Peace Commission, a high-level commission for compliance verification, and spokespersons from the M-19, the Communist Party, and the EPL, Popular Liberation Army, the Ejército Popular de Liberación.

He was choking on his words, he was so angry. But he read on: The government called all popular and armed groups to join in dialogues to extend the ceasefire to all groups and find ways to make the changes the country so desperately needed.

"This new president is a complete idiot!" Colonel Restrepo shouted. "Who does he think he is? He can't repeal the Security Statute and lift the state of emergency!"

Ricardo was throwing things now, yelling and swearing. And then he became very quiet and put his head in his hands. "What are we going to do?" he murmured finally. "Norma, tell me, what are we going to do?"

The Security Statute had been working well for the past two administrations; it funded the military for overtime pay and gave it complete autonomy to maintain the rule of law, however it deemed necessary. Bogotá was buzzing with complaints that the president had overstepped his authority when he ordered military leaders to obey him as commander in chief of the armed forces. The power of the rank was vested in the head of state by the Constitution, but as a formality; it had always been left in practice to top military leaders.

Every branch of the armed forces adamantly disagreed with the amnesty, with freeing the prisoners, and with the privileges offered to the former revolutionaries as they were reinserted into civil society. But the president ignored them. He even went a step further and bragged to the media that he had finally done what Héctor Osuna's cartoon in the *Espectador* newspaper had done, and "put on his boots." He was ready.

The thing was, Ricardo was a colonel in the army and chief of the military brigade. He had no choice but to obey and to carry out his superiors' orders. He had to free the political prisoners in the Antioquia prisons and set up reinsertion offices for logistical support as they returned to civilian life.

The first thing he did was go talk to his sister, the director of the Buen Pastor. The amnesty covered Miguel's mother. That afternoon Madre Susana appeared at their door in nearly the same state as her brother: utterly shocked and outraged. But she was different. She knew how to exercise self-control. Her stoicism made her unflappable.

Like Ricardo, Madre Susana vehemently disagreed with the peace policy; she thought it could only bring more chaos to the country.

"How can we trust those delinquents dressed up in revolutionary costumes? They have nerve to use their social cause to justify whatever they do. Political prisoners are worse than common criminals," she declared categorically. "In the end, criminals are sorry for what they did. But that is not true for those who call themselves revolutionaries. If it were up to me, they would get the death penalty."

That afternoon she recalled in great detail when the throngs of guerrilleras began arriving at the prison during the repression. She had had no qualms whatsoever as she launched a ruthless offensive against them. She hounded them in interrogations, forcing them to contradict themselves by denying their crimes and then begging for pardon. The muchachas protested passionately, but then she would threaten to cut off their visits and ration their food. She also banned them from the radio and TV. At one point, she declared that there was no such thing as political crime. That was how she turned the mere mention of their groups' initials or their political slogans into contempt of her authority.

She recounted how she snuck up on them gathered in a cell listening to protest songs by Mercedes Sosa and Atahualpa Yupanqui. She took great pleasure in confiscating the tape recorder and cassettes, and she gave them all a week in isolation. The prisoners' response was to sing Sosa at the top of their lungs every single day that week: "¡*Si se calla el cantor, calla la vida!*"

What made her happiest was forcing them to go to daily Mass and, on top of that, to say the rosary and go to confession every Sunday. She made them go through the rituals, not because she wanted to convert them to the truth of religious doctrine, but because she wanted to break them. She knew her methods were questionable. She didn't use physical violence, but she got the same results. She undermined their dignity and crushed their spirits. She didn't use that technique with all prisoners; it was only the political prisoners, she said with fierce pride. She would have gladly sentenced them all to life in prison. And now she had to set them free, even though it went against the very fiber of her being.

The thorniest point was Miguel's mamá. The amnesty covered her, and she would obviously want her son back. Ricardo tried to convince his sister to authorize legal adoption, to invent some reason and prove the mother unfit.

"How can you even entertain the thought that after having Miguel for two years, we are going to let anyone take him away?" said Ricardo. "What will happen to him in that woman's hands? She won't ever leave her life of crime. If you don't want to do it for us, think about the boy and what this will mean to him."

Madre Susana refused to promise anything. "I thought that in ordinary circumstances the prisoner would have had at least five more years to serve, and a lot could happen in that time. The boy could grow to love his adopted family, and he himself would refuse to go with a woman he didn't even know. But it is too soon for that, and the law provides no guidance in these cases. As is to be expected, given my position and my responsibilities, I prefer to keep everything within the law. This is out of my hands."

Then I chimed in. "When I agreed to take Miguel, I did it with the clear understanding that he would be considered our son. This is how we have lived all this time. I have come to consider him my own son, and I refuse to give him back to a woman who most likely didn't even want him, and for whom he must be a burden and a bother. She can have a lot more children. In her world, they all have hordes of children."

31

I lit a cigarette; my hands were trembling. I saw that Ricardo's face was beet-red. His stance was crystal clear.

"Norma and I have taken on Miguel as our son, and there is not even a remote possibility that we will let him go. The muchacho stays. That is final!"

Although Ricardo didn't go on to say this, we all understood anyway: Miguel had saved our marriage. My family clearly saw Ricardo as an opportunist who had curried favor through his distinguished military career. How many obstacles had he had to face, to climb the ladder in the hierarchy of an institution where family background mattered as much as social standing? He was an orphan, so he had none of those advantages. He had to demonstrate his talent as an exemplary soldier through perseverance, will, and stoicism. Part of his strategy was to marry me, for the social position. I was aware of that and was fine with it. My motives didn't have a lot to do with love, either—I was afraid of being single forever. We had a tacit agreement to maintain the appearance of a harmonious marriage. Still, his lack of sophistication and his coarseness irritated me tremendously. I didn't care that he was not a creative lover; you can learn to live with that—but you can't live with social embarrassment. In the last few years our relationship had become so distant that it was unbearable. Miguel arrived at a crucial point in our married life and saved us from certain separation.

But this issue was more delicate than divorce. My parents would not condone the social disgrace of having my son taken away, and even less under the murky circumstances of his adoption. My whole family and all my close friends had swallowed my story that the child had been legally adopted. They had no clue about Miguel's real background. If they had had any inkling of it, they never would have condoned such a sordid arrangement.

◎

The nun left, but no agreement had been reached. They were obviously not going to back down, and she found herself between a rock and a hard place. That explained her warning as she left: "Remember, the child bears the mark of Cain. You won't be able to save him from that, no matter how hard you try."

Undecided

Amparo

Contigo mi vida quiero vivir la vida y lo que me queda de vida, quiero vivir contigo . . . I hummed Shakira's "Mi vida" this morning as I went from table to table shaking my money-maker like Shakira does hers. I was just finishing up with the customers when I saw my compañera Cristina coming up to the juice stand.

I treated her to a *jugo de lulo* and some *empanadas*, and we sat down to chat.

"You've been flighty since the party last Saturday, Amparo. Tell me what's going on."

"Oh, amiga, they are both a little off! One keeps coming by the stand and goes to sit under the ceiba tree, watching me. The other spends all his time in don Eusebio's shop with his crew and doesn't say all that much. But I can tell he watches me all the time. And as for me, well, they've both got a hold on me. I can't decide. I want them both because—it's the weirdest thing—they seem so alike, even if they're so different. You know what I mean?"

"Well, yeah, you're all giddy because they're paying attention to you. But do you even know who they are? You must be careful. You never know who is who."

"And have you ever sat down to think about what chances we have to find a man here in Podunk? Don't you think for one second that I'm going to be scared off by anyone. Besides, Mono, or whatever his name is, is from here. He showed me his mamá's place. And he told me he goes to school in Medellín; he comes to visit every now and then."

"And the other guy?"

"He is a little odd. I heard them call him 'Comandante.' He must be in the brigade."

"You are so incredibly naive! Not all comandantes are in the army. There haven't been any men from the brigade in this village for years. Be careful. You

33

are going to get yourself into trouble. The fact that neither one stops by the juice stand or visits you at home makes me very uneasy."

"You know what? Just shut up, you're starting to get on my nerves. You are just as paranoid as all the rest."

I got up and left Cristina sitting there; her words and her empanada both stuck in her mouth.

It made me mad. I knew Cristina was right. But I was seventeen, and that was the furthest thing from my mind. I knew I was pretty, and I felt like I was wasting my youth in that god-forsaken village. What did I have to look forward to? Farmers and villagers. My school compañeras were conservative and hypocritical. I dreamed of getting out of there, going to Miami, becoming rich and famous. Truth be told, I wanted to be famous. I'd be a beauty queen first, move up to television news anchor, and then be an actress. I spent hours in front of the mirror, striking the poses I saw models and actresses do on TV. Someone had to get me out of there. So I set my sights on the non-townies. If possible, non-Colombians. When the oil company was exploring the area, I saw my ticket out. But I was too young, and the company didn't last long with all the kidnapping threats toward the engineers. That's when I started to keep an eye open for any new face. In the meantime, I kind of liked being the center of attention.

Of course, my father yelled at me and warned me that I had to be careful with outsiders. But there was no way I was going to listen to him! Anyway, he was busy with his job as police chief and had other things on his mind. Every night it was the same thing at home. My parents sat down to watch the news and then have endless debates: the demilitarized zone in the south was an idiotic idea from that stupid conservative president of ours; Plan Colombia was a gringo charade to prop up the military. "Two billion dollars? Honey, you know how much that is? All that money poured into weapons they say are for the war on drugs! And where does all that *dinero* go? To the army? No! To line the pockets of the paramilitaries, the damn *paracos*! As if we needed more weapons!" And over and over again with "if the Peace Commission would just stop playing along with Tirofijo and Mono Jojoy." And the tired old refrain: "The guerrillas have taken over the country while all us civil authorities sit here with our arms crossed!" It was all blah-blah-blah! And the only thing that I cared about was watching *Ugly Betty* in peace. "Shut up already!" I would yell. After a while I gave up. I shut myself off in my room with my earbuds stuck in my ears, trying to escape from a reality that I saw as lightyears away. And I fantasized about having the life that every girl my age dreams of.

Freedom

Mariate

"Freedom! Freedom!" block-eight prisoners shouted for joy and hugged each other. "Long live the revolution! Time for social justice! The people for the people! Progress or death! Up with the ELN! Down with the oligarchy and imperialism!"

I couldn't believe it. Even though I had never had a trial, let alone been proven guilty, I was freed under the government's amnesty for political prisoners. We read the press release, and I still had a hard time believing it. We were granted immediate release and other benefits: funds to start up a small business, housing assistance for those in the reinsertion process, and even academic scholarships. The new president wanted to make up for all the repression of his predecessor. His policy opened the door for revolutionaries to negotiate and talk about their demands at the table.

Nora gave me a bear hug and asked if I wanted to join the ELN right away.

"You know I have to find my son. That's my priority."

"You know how and where to find us. The struggle continues, compañera. We are going to savor our freedom," responded Nora.

"You? Really? The one who doesn't believe anything having to do with the government? I thought you would never accept amnesty. Don't you say it's just another control mechanism used by the Establishment?" I challenged, joking.

"You're right, sardina. I am an anarchist and a skeptic. But I'm no idiot."

Other prisoners did not share the joy flooding through the prison. Most thought it was unfair for people doing time for rioting, kidnapping, and attempted murder, people who had caused innocent people to die, to go free while they wasted away in prison for petty crimes they had committed for sheer survival. Those of us covered by the amnesty tried to shake off our guilt;

we told them that the goal of the armed struggle was to give future generations a better country.

"We're going to build a new country, one that has no poverty and no inequity, one that has opportunity for everyone!" we shouted.

◎

Mariate had to stay in prison for several more days to get a meeting with Madre Superiora who, for some reason or other, was always busy or gone, in meetings or otherwise unavailable. When Madre finally deigned to meet with her, Mariate tried to tamp down her excitement and nerves when she asked about Miguel. The nun was evasive. Since the child had been placed in the care of a family for the past two and a half years, Mariate would have to prove to the Instituto Bienestar Familiar that she was his legal mother, that she could support him and give him a good life, one that was comparable to the one he had now. She could not believe it. There were literally hundreds of poor kids running around, and no one cared about them! Doesn't the Instituto Bienestar Familiar want to help them? According to Madre Superiora, a child born in prison had precriminal behavior that could be reprogrammed if he had the opportunity to grow up in a healthy environment.

Madre changed her tone when she saw how desperate Mariate was. She told her not to worry. She could get her son back as soon as she got back to a normal family life with her husband—because, of course, her marriage was fully recognized by the Catholic Church, right? When they were both well positioned to present the required documentation, and when her husband could of course prove he made a living wage and was a law-abiding citizen, there would be no problem for her to get her son back.

Madre herself had recorded the birth of the baby in the prison. She should have those records. But when Mariate asked, the nun flatly denied it. As far as being married by the Catholic Church, well, no, of course she wasn't. He was her husband, but not with all the legalities that the nun demanded. So she could not prove a thing. She was completely powerless. All her arguments were in vain. It was all up to Madre; it all depended on the director. And Madre now denied the existence of the birth record and thereby Mariate's right to have her son.

Madre Superiora turned a deaf ear to Mariate's pleas and protests. There was no way to appeal this sentence.

◎

"If you want to get out of prison, this is the path to freedom. Of course, if you prefer to wait, you can continue to serve your time. That is your choice. And my advice is that you forget about this. You will have more children, I am sure. You are young, and you have your whole life ahead of you. Be careful, though— don't continue down your path of crime. I know you are not as unruly as the others—though I strongly recommend that you cut off your friendship with that Nora. That muchacha is not good for you. And you should feel very fortunate that your child is being raised in the best possible conditions. His family loves him dearly, and the boy is happy with them. What can you give him? Really. Tell me. What can you, fresh out of prison, offer a two-year-old boy? Think about him and about what is best for him."

"At least tell me who has him and how I can see him and talk to them, to explain my situation," I pleaded.

The nun was resolute. She could not divulge that information. There was nothing left she could do. But something deep inside me stirred. What could I give him? I would pick up that gauntlet she had thrown down. Oh, yes. I would take that path to freedom, and I would dedicate my life to finding my son, to getting him back. Even if I had to steal, resort to a life of crime, or confront the entire judicial system. I was going to find Julián, and together we would do it. Prison had taught us how to survive.

Before I left her office, I told Madre Superiora in no uncertain terms: "I swear I will dedicate my whole life to getting my son back, even if I have to pay for it by coming back to these prison walls."

Madre looked at me blankly but didn't dignify my words with a response.

Patria Potestad
Norma

Miguel was three now and just about ready for preschool. Norma was busy gathering the paperwork she needed to get him into one of Medellín's best schools. She had to submit his personal information along with medical and psychiatric certificates to prove he was emotionally ready and had age-appropriate motor skills. She spent hours making appointments with doctors, psychologists, and specialists, all to prove that a three-year-old was ready to go to preschool.

◎

"Don't touch those papers, Miguel!" I groaned.

"I don't want to go to school," he whined.

"Every child has to go to school," I said, unconvinced, leafing through the papers I had to submit by next Friday at the latest. His constant questions and chatter made me jittery.

"I don't want to go to the doctor, Mamá."

"Miguelito, can't you see I'm busy? Give me a minute to get these papers together! What do I need? What do I need? Of course. No surprise. The birth certificate."

◎

Her husband was supposed to be getting the birth certificate. She didn't know whether he would be able to get it by Friday. And that would be a serious complication. How could San Ignacio School admit a child with no birth certificate? It wouldn't happen. And the baptismal certificate? Had he even been baptized? All those details had been put off, and Ricardo got mad at her every time she asked him about it. Now, since Miguel was so close to starting school, Ricardo couldn't dodge the issue. He had to take care of it.

What Norma did not know was that her husband was not able to give her the birth certificate because it simply did not exist. Madre Superiora at the Buen Pastor prison had confessed that when he was born in the prison, she, the presiding authority, had recorded the birth but had never submitted the paperwork. She had figured that she would give his mother the papers when she got out of prison, and the young woman would take care of it. But things had taken a different turn. The prison paper recording the birth was the only evidence there was of the event. And now that three years had gone by, it was doubly complicated. By law, if a birth was not registered within a certain time frame, there had to be a hearing.

Thursday night, Ricardo came home and finally gave Norma an official birth certificate, duly submitted, recording the legal adoption of Miguel Restrepo Alvarez by the Restrepo family at the age of six months, after the death of his biological mother.

◉

"His mother died?" I asked doubtfully.

"Affirmative," he responded, standing as if at attention.

I could tell by the tone of his voice that I should not ask. I preferred not to know, not to get involved in the details. I felt that way about anything that had to do with the circles in which my husband moved. So I turned to scrutinize the certificate and saw something that seemed much easier to answer.

"Wasn't his full name Miguel Angel? You forgot his middle name."

"And what if I did?" he retorted, irate. "After all I have had to go through, the only thing you can see is that minute detail? I don't even like the name Angel."

"I do, kind of," I said off-handedly.

One week later we learned that Madre Superiora had resigned as director of the Buen Pastor prison. My husband was not surprised at the news, but he refused to talk about it. From that point, he and his sister were more distant. I was always curious about what went on when they met in the prison just days before we registered Miguel at the Jesuit school. I had a feeling that it was all connected to Miguel's situation. But back then, appearances mattered more to me than what happened behind the scenes. My husband took care of all the dirty laundry.

The Threat

Amparo

When Amparo got home that afternoon, the house was full. Her dad was meeting with some of San Juan's bigwigs. Any other night she would have headed straight up to her room and not even looked twice at the group, but tonight her mom asked her to help with the food, and the discussion was so heated that she couldn't help but listen in.

"We don't have a choice. They will get what they want, with or without our cooperation. Plenty of people in this village would love to earn a few pesos in exchange for some information. If we don't work with them, we put ourselves smack-dab in the line of fire. There is no middle ground here: We are either for them or against them. And it is in our best interest to be for them. I like knowing they're going to take care of the guerrillas crawling all over the countryside. Ranchers haven't been able to get to their *fincas* for a while now; parcels have either been abandoned or taken over by guerrillas. The paramilitaries are the only ones who can scare the guerrilla forces."

"What price, don Mariano? What's the cost?" my papá, the chief, shouted, exasperated. "Do you know how those guys do what they do? Half the village has some connection or other to the guerrillas; everyone knows that. They even backed you when you ran for mayor! It is the only way to survive. We don't agree with it, but that's how it is. The paracos are merciless. It will be utter massacre. I say we don't give them the information they want, and we hang on to as much dignity as we can."

"I disagree," the mayor countered, cutting off the chief. "We don't have any way to defend ourselves, and they are going to come for us first. Think this over, Chief."

41

"This is not just about the ranchers. It's also about the regular people who own smaller plots of land; they are the ones who'll fall into these guys' hands. You know what has happened in other villages—innocent people butchered just because they're caught in the middle. You are the head of the village, I am the head of public safety, and it is our responsibility not to allow that to happen here."

"And what do you suggest we do? Ask the brigade for help? It's not going to come. It'd be just the opposite! It is entirely too easy for them if the paras take on the guerrillas. Or even better, we ask the guerrillas for help? Either way we have a massacre," Mayor Mariano responded haughtily.

Then there was silence, and it was long. And uncomfortable. The air was steamy in the afternoon sun, and it hung heavy. I watched from the dining room out of the corner of my eye, as they all tried to mop up the sweat soaking their shirts and dripping down their foreheads and necks. The whirring of the fan blades in constant motion was the only sound. Just then my mamá told me to help her pass around a tray of *jugo de maracuyá*. The drink was timely and refreshing, and helped them regain composure and clear their heads. No one said thank you or even noticed I was there. One of the policemen broke the silence.

"We should help them find the guerrilla commando camping over by Valdivia. That way they blow each other up and we don't have the bloodshed in the village."

"Do you have any idea what you're saying?" Papá interrupted. "That would be giving them carte blanche to take justice into their own hands and basically telling them that we, the ones in charge of law and order, are incapable of doing it ourselves. And how many people in town have kids or other relatives in that camp? Or did you forget all the guerrilla recruitment campaigns around?"

The mayor jumped to respond, and nearly everyone there agreed with him: "What police department with limited, obsolete, standard-issue weapons can take on a guerrilla commando with state-of-the-art weapons and troops? It goes without saying that we can't stand up to the paras—their weapons are better than the guerrillas'. I think we should join the paras because no matter what, with or without our help, they will get what they are after. Standing up to them is a death sentence for the entire village. Think about it, Chief."

The debate came to an end with no agreement reached. Some got up and left in defiance, along with the mayor. My papá dropped his head into his hands and said to the few who remained: "I won't let anyone turn in any of our villagers. That would be tantamount to sentencing them to death. I am not going to support or agree to any attack by cooperating with an illegal armed group. I will not tolerate any lack of respect for authority. We represent the law in this town, and we are going to make sure it is respected with what little we have and, above all, with our dignity intact."

It had been three years since my papá, don Luciano López came to San Juan as its new police chief. He had been working as a police officer for several years in Sabaneta, but during the terrifying reign of Pablo Escobar, he had asked for a transfer to somewhere more peaceful, to raise his children in a better place. He never imagined that the farther he went from the city, the more danger there would be. They had escaped the Medellín Cartel that disbanded after Pablo Escobar's death and had run right into the battle to the death between the paras and the guerrillas.

When everyone had left, my papá called my mother, my brother, and me to the dining room table and told us what had happened. They had learned some paras were in town a few days earlier. It was easy to spot them. But that week what they had feared would happen, did happen. The leader of the paramilitaries had contacted him and asked for help identifying people who collaborated with the guerrillas. He had been specific; he did not mean help identifying the leaders. They knew who they were. They wanted the people who were supplying them, who were information runners. It was part of their strategy in every village: to intimidate the villagers so they would do as they were told, and then to cut off the guerrillas' logistical support. They picked out a few they suspected were collaborators and murdered them as an example to force everyone else to sing. The paras assumed the local authorities would back them, and it didn't really matter if they didn't, because they didn't have a choice. No police department had the weapons or the forces to stand up to them. When Papá told his superiors about the paras' threat, they said all the villages were in the same boat. They had to make do with what they had. In other words, cave in. My mamá started to pray, and all I could do was go up to my room and throw myself on my bed, my CD player blaring against my ears. I had figured out that our little world was tumbling down. Maybe the noise would be loud enough to numb my senses, and I could shut myself off from a reality that I had until then viewed as distant. The truth was, I was terrified, just like everyone else in the village.

Light and Shadow

Mariate

Four years stretch into eternity when you're living the hell of torture. I barely recognized Julián when we were finally reunited. We looked at each other; there were no words between us. Something was different—there was a tinge of sorrow, of deep desolation, that would forever be a part of us now.

Yet despite all those changes, our bodies remembered. All we had to do was touch and the dams broke. We were drenched in the desire we'd been holding back for so long. My pores opened one by one all over my body as my skin recalled textures and caresses, exposing emotions I'd repressed for years. A torrent of passion came bursting through, and we clung to each other in the flood, checking our impatience as we drowned countless nights of loneliness and bitterness in our love. How we'd missed each other! We climaxed together, tangled up in prolonged moans. I wanted to stop time at that very moment. Julián! Julián! Finally, Julián was in our bed—the same bed we'd been torn from four long, painful years ago.

I lost myself in his arms. It was when I was resting my head against his chest that I saw his scars from the torture. I asked him about it. "You don't want to know," he responded dryly. He was curious about other things.

"What happened with the baby?"

"It has been a never-ending battle! It's even worse now that I'm out of prison. Madre Superiora never answers my calls, and I can't do anything without her."

"Well, there is something we can do," he reasoned. "We can get a little information and take back what is ours. There is legal recourse."

He had learned a little about the law and how to give grounds for claims in prison. His words gave me hope.

"If you help me, we could get all the documents they want! We could get married, get the birth certificate, go to Bienestar Familiar . . . If we must, we can get a lawyer. They can't deny us that."

"Yes, they can. While they have the control and the power, they can do whatever they want," he said.

There was legal recourse, but Julián understood that we were outsiders in that society and we didn't have the money to take them on. Our prison records didn't help, either. It was awful, but something as natural as getting our son back was out of reach for us.

"Don't worry. There are other ways," said Julián. He already had everything figured out.

"*Negra, mi amor*, I'm sure my compañeros will help us track him down and amp up the pressure on his adoptive parents. First, we have to find out who has him. What we do know is that someone with a lot of power is behind this. Madre Superiora said a relative of hers has him? We just have to find out who. That is our starting point."

I felt safe in Julián's arms. He would take care of it. I wasn't alone anymore. We would do it together. He was more mature now, sure of his mission in life. He'd become a man. I held tightly to him. My jet-black mane cascaded over his chest of curly, chestnut hair. The mid-afternoon light filtered in through the roof and sketched our silhouettes on the wall: light and shadow become fire.

◔

Julián and Mariate had met at school in their hometown of Marinilla. They'd been together since Mariate was fourteen. It might never have gone any further than a school crush, except her father was the authoritarian type who turned into a monster every time he had too much to drink. Then he took it out on his children. One day she got fed up with it and left home to go live with Julián. At first, she thought it would be temporary, just until things calmed down at home. But little by little she adapted to a couple's life, and before long she was pregnant. He was her first and only love. Things might not ever have changed if Julián hadn't decided to help his friend and hide the weapons, even though he had no idea where they'd come from. But digging into the past did no good now. They were together again. Early on, life had given them the chance to taste human misery in all its glory. Starting now, things would be different. Like starting over.

They settled into housing assigned by the reinsertion office, and Mariate spent her time trying to find a job as a maid. Once she had regular houses to clean three days a week, she turned her attention to looking for Miguel.

Before she got out of prison, she had found out Madre Superiora had a brother in the army. This confidential tidbit had slipped out of the only nun who'd shown her any compassion: the little sister with whom she embroidered and crocheted. She was the one who'd told her about the colonel's visits to Madre. So Mariate began to research high-society families in the military elite. There was no sorrow in her search anymore; she didn't complain. Instead, she was fiercely determined—she had learned that much through all the ups and downs in her short life.

Before long, Julián's compañeros contacted him again. He had to report to the M-19 high command to begin intensive training for a top-secret mission.

◎

"But the amnesty still holds, right?" I protested angrily when he told me he had orders to go, but he couldn't tell me where.

"Amnesty is a figure of speech," he replied with conviction. "You think the army will let this ceasefire go on for much longer? Let the reinserted get all those benefits the government announced? The commando has to be ready for anything, and even if there is a quote-unquote truce, we don't have true conditions for peace yet."

"Julián, we said that our number-one priority was to get Miguel back. How are we going to prove that we can give him a stable family life? Besides, you get amnesty benefits, too, right?"

Julián was silent for a bit, then said simply: "I'm sure that wherever they send me, I'll be able to do a lot more from there than what we could do by taking the legal route. Give me some time. You'll see."

"Then I'm going with you. I can get back in touch with Nora and my *combo* friends from the ELN. They will take me in with no questions asked."

"Don't even think about it. I need you here, heading up our home. You will be my link to a family and a future, the stable future we want to give our kids. Right? If you go with them, you will be just one more woman prostituting herself in the guerrillas. I don't want you to be my compañera in war; I want you to be my wife at home."

"A wife at home is worth more than a compañera in the fight?" I asked. But I got no answer. Julián had just conferred on me the role of wife, the refuge

47

for the guerrillero, which denied me the right to be part of the revolution. The injustice in what he had said was obvious. But I didn't dare bring it completely out into the light, at least not then. Because I wasn't convinced I wanted to leave the relative peace I'd found to go on the hunt for more hardship. Julián left for who knows where, and shortly after that, I found out I was pregnant with our second child.

Muerte a secuestradores! MAS!
Death to Kidnappers!
Norma

Ricardo surprised Norma and invited her to a cattle hacienda in Puerto Berrío. He almost never asked her to go with him to business events. But this time he needed her to showcase his social position.

There were quite a few ranchers from the area there, including the manager of the livestock rancher foundation Fondo Ganadero, who owned a vast tract of land where more than a thousand head of cattle grazed; the *rejoneo* bullfighter Norberto Pabón, well known for his shady business deals and connections with the Medellín Cartel; and some conservative *caciques* from Antioquia. Norma knew she was in for a long afternoon of boring conversation about maids, children, or cheating spouses, while she waited for some juicy gossip to drop. But that day the men launched a civilized discussion that escalated in tone and tenor until it had spiraled down into a shouting match, complete with insults. She was afraid her husband would unleash his usual crass humor, and so she placed herself where she could hear what filtered out from the living room.

"You all know we are very concerned about what is going on in the region; we have decided to put the brakes on the guerrillas. We cannot allow them to continue to intimidate us or take over our land with absolutely no consequences. We want to know whether the army can help us fight these thugs or whether we should act on our own," declared Pabón.

"The government has a comprehensive peace policy. It is soft on the guerrillas. Both of those factors have tied the armed forces' hands," Colonel Restrepo retorted defensively.

"It is unconscionable for these criminals to be free to harass us and crush our economy!" the Fondo Ganadero manager complained.

José Echeverría, one of the important caciques in the region, joined in angrily: "Our haciendas are collapsing around us. We can't take care of our animals; guerrilleros go in and out whenever they feel like it; they rustle our cattle every single day. The last time I was at the ranch, a FARC, the Fuerzas Armadas Revolucionarias de Colombia (Revolutionary Armed Forces of Colombia) column showed up in the middle of the night, shoved us up against the wall with our hands on our heads, and threatened to kidnap my thirteen- and fifteen-year-olds if we didn't hand over a whole herd of calves. We haven't been able to go back since."

"What're we going to do? Just let them run us off?" the bullfighter Pabón took advantage of the collective anger and pressed on. "Let them steal our ranches and turn us out of our homes? What's next? Will they be able to throw us out of our city and take over the country while we sit on our hands?"

"What should we do, don Norberto?" several men asked. Everyone turned to see what he would say next.

"The only thing left to do," said don Norberto, "is to come together and declare war on those bastards, show them who has more power and more balls. They threaten us? So, we burn them. There is no middle ground here. But we all have to be in this together, there can be no wishy-washiness, no doubt. You already know I can take care of operations, but I still need your help. I need you ranchers for financial support and the colonel for logistical support, especially on the military side of things. Anyone who's a member of the Antioquian clubs can help raise community support so that word doesn't get out. This last point is especially important. For example, I would love to be a member of the Unión de Medellín Club, but so far . . . Still, if Señor Echeverría backs me and a few of my compañeros for seats on the board, you and yours can go back to your ranches worry-free; you don't have to know how things get done. Are you in or out?"

They all looked at each other, clearing their throats and faking coughs. They knew if they said yes to Señor Pabón, they were okaying his illegal activities and would be at the mercy of the narco-traffickers. The guerrillas wouldn't control the area, the narcos would. Of the two evils, the latter guaranteed access to their ranches and therefore economic and social power. But what was the price? Ricardo, summoning all the experience his military rank had given him, thought about his next move. Would he be jeopardizing his career and position by supporting this?

"I cannot speak for the military," he said. "What I say here, I say for me personally. If I work with you, it will be on a personal basis. And I will try to keep the army from getting in your way. That is all I can do."

"Don't worry, my dear Ricardo. May I call you Ricardo, are we on a first-name basis now?" said don Norberto somewhat sarcastically. "We have had the support of the armed forces guaranteed for some time. Don't you know I have connections with General Vega in the capital? The general has already promised me he will grant us, shall we say, special impunity. And here we have the backing of the Castaño brothers, who provide training and operational support. We are the ones who put up the funds."

It was clear that even if the military command wasn't participating actively, it had given carte blanche to the civilian groups taking justice into their own hands. The state could not guarantee the defense and safety of its citizens. Since people needed to defend themselves against the guerrillas, self-defense groups had been springing up throughout the country. Little by little they were gaining strength.

On the way back to Medellin, I tried to talk to my husband about what I had just heard, but he shut me down.

"You keep your nose out of this; this is men's business," he responded flatly. Silence was the rule in our relationship. Again.

I wasn't surprised when I started seeing signs and graffiti plastered here and there on the walls along the streets in cities and towns:

LONG LIVE MAS: DEATH TO KIDNAPPERS!

Persecution

Amparo

B odies began to appear, bobbing up and down in the river.
Comandante didn't find it particularly challenging that San Juan as a village openly accepted the guerrillas and allowed them to control the town. But the chief's attitude irritated him, as did his flat refusal to support the extermination campaign. The guerrillas were quiet. Everyone knew they were camped out on the Valdivia side of town, but so far they had been still.

Rumors from nearby villages came tumbling in. The paramilitary had launched a siege in Córdoba and was tightening it more and more as the bands operating in the zone gained ground. Hordes of displaced people moved from town to town in search of peace. Teachers began to be targets of intimidation or murder for belonging to one political party or another, and soon both elementary and high schools were completely deserted. Even if teachers weren't personally targeted, they were traumatized and fled, hauling what little they had with them.

Amparo pretended she didn't know what was going on. It was easy to close herself off in her little world. She went from her house to school in the morning, then to the limonada stand where she helped her mamá, then home at night. Her father said they all had to be at home by nine every night. The world outside those doors ceased to exist.

She saw Comandante again around the stand, with his rear guard ever in tow. Their relationship had stalled at flirting and smiles, always from a distance. She wished and wished he would make the next move, but he didn't budge. He'd built up a wall, and no one could penetrate it.

At the same time, Mono had become downright persistent. He called all the time, left her little notes, and came by on weekends. They went to the movies a couple of times, but always in secret. He wouldn't go to her house and always dropped her off on the corner of her street. He was very careful not to be seen in public. If they went to the movies, they always met inside. Amparo could not understand the need for so much secrecy. When he was relaxed, he was loving and tender. He loved to joke around, and he made her laugh with his one-liners.

One afternoon, as I was serving drinks to a table, I overheard the customers' conversation: "Mayor Mariano has sided with the paras. He gave them a list of people he says work with the guerrillas. The chief of police is on the list. Now we are really in their hands. There's nothing we can do."

That night I told my father. He listened and didn't seem upset, as if he had known all about the list. He did call another family meeting, though.

"Things are turning really nasty in the village," he said. "I was afraid this would happen, and it has. I have asked for protection and help from my superiors, but all they give me is lots of excuses and no hope. We have to defend ourselves as best we can. We need to be on guard. You kids, you have to be very careful. We don't know what is going to happen, but hard times are on the horizon."

The Second Angel
Mariate

Mariate named her second son Gabriel Angel, after the archangel messenger of God. He came right when she needed him to help counter the deep ache in her heart after losing her first baby, and to offset how lonely and desperate she felt. Julián left, and she moved in with her sister Jacinta in the Betania barrio of northeastern Medellín. Jacinta minded the baby while Mariate went to work. And yes, of course, Julián called a lot and would even show up now and then, but that was not being a husband. It wasn't anything, really. Mariate was young and pretty, and would have gladly traded her fate of profound solitude and not knowing where her man was, for that of any other woman with her man at home.

Gabriel grew healthy and strong. He had inherited his grandfather's green eyes and Julián's chestnut hair. His face was sweet, innocent and impish. Mariate was still working as a maid in the Medellín neighborhood of El Poblado, hoping against hope she would one day find Miguel there. She had also started to tap into amnesty benefits while they were available. She wanted to study microbusiness and social services at the national learning center, SENA, but first she had to finish high school. She made a rigid schedule and got up every morning at five to work on her distance classes through the Sutatenza radio high school program. Finally, high school diploma in hand, she was admitted to SENA. She never missed a single night class, even though she was exhausted after working all day, every day.

All the paperwork, all her legwork and appearances before family law attorneys and judges and recorder's offices and law offices had been useless. The child and family service Instituto Bienestar Familiar required her to prove her relation to Miguel, and she simply didn't have the documentation. She told her story again and again in office after office, ministry after ministry. The response never varied: "Come back tomorrow" or "There's nothing we can do" or "Get a lawyer" or "You need to bring a witness . . ." There were plenty of witnesses, but they were active ELN guerrilleras, and there was absolutely no way they would be allowed to testify. Mariate had even appealed to the Office of the First Lady, through the so-called Solidarity programs that always touted her good works with the less fortunate. At first, one assistant actually listened to her. The woman found her case intriguing because it was so unusual, and she contacted the prison and the Ministry of Justice. Then they found out that Miguel had been adopted by a high-ranking military official, and Mariate was quickly dismissed with very polite pretexts, her hope dashed yet again. After that, no was the norm, and she finally understood that it had never been about documentation or proving family relation. It was about where she was on the social ladder. It was impossible to fight the system from the outcast rung.

When she had time off, her favorite thing to do was watch Gabriel play and jibber-jabber in the singsong paisa way. He was growing to be a true-blue Antioquian. He was the one who inspired her to get an education and move forward—not by doing what Julián did in running off to the mountains to fight, but by setting an example and staying with Gabriel to help him become someone. She wanted to get ahead so she could offer both of her boys a better life, so when she found Miguel and showed him she was his real mother, he wouldn't be ashamed of her. He was almost five, and she figured he must be big now and getting into everything; he was probably constantly on the move and curious like his father, and sweet and loving like she herself was. She would daydream of them meeting by chance. Oh, she would hug him tight to her and cover him with kisses! And she wondered what he would do.

Nothing positive had happened on the legal front of her fight to get her son back, but her search had not been completely in vain. She had followed the trails of so many military families that finally a compañera put her in touch with a lady who worked for the Restrepo family in the Poblado area. Her name was Carmen, and she worked in the Los Guaduales condominium complex. Her boss was an army colonel and his last name was Restrepo, just like Madre Superiora's. Half of Antioquia had that last name, but Mariate's gut told her this was the one. She got to talk to Carmen one Sunday afternoon while out and about, and that was when she finally landed a lead on the trail that she'd been following for so long. It wasn't easy. Carmen was reserved and tight-lipped. But after talking and talking, the stitchery work Mariate had in her bag caught Carmen's eye.

◉

"You do needlework?" asked Carmen.

"Which one do you like? Look, I have little jackets here, scarves, baby bonnets. I sell them in boutiques and stores, and people can order them, too. I also embroider on sheets, tablecloths, linens . . ."

Carmen examined the bag of needlework and pulled out a little hooded ruana. She looked it over carefully, looked at me from head to toe, and then something in her attitude changed. From then on, she was nice and chatty.

"Señora Norma is so stressed right now with little Miguel's birthday coming up next week. She's running us all ragged with work. She told us not to even ask to take a day off next weekend."

My legs were trembling, but I held it together and as casually as I could, I asked, "And how old is the boy . . . Miguel?"

"He'll be five," said Carmen. "He is right at the age when kids are a handful, and on top of that he is spoiled rotten. Sometimes even I can't stand to be around him."

I bit my lip so I wouldn't start screaming. Little Miguel would be five on November 9. It was my son, right there, within reach! But I had to keep calm. I did my best to sound indifferent and said, "Carmen, look, I've been looking for a job. Do you know if they need any help in the house? Someone to wash clothes or iron?"

"Oh, I don't recommend it at all, honey! This family is really demanding. He's in the army and they're on high alert. I stay because I've been with the señora for years. The colonel is always surrounded by bodyguards. That boy can't even go to the park without guards. They are so overprotective. I'm the one who spends the most time with him, but he doesn't listen to me because they let him do whatever he wants. They never tell that child no."

Carmen went on and on with details about the family's habits, how the boy was spoiled, how many toy guns he had, and how he drove her crazy with all his noise.

"If I didn't love the little squirt so much—I mean, I've raised him since he was tiny—I swear I'd be out of there," she said.

"You've raised him since he was born?" I asked.

Here Carmen became more cautious; she could feel the emotion behind the question and so steered the conversation in a different direction.

"Well, the truth is, I can't really complain because the señora treats us well; she is demanding, but generous."

I could feel Carmen getting suspicious. I kept asking questions, but I was more careful, even if my face betrayed my joy. Until she stopped me short.

"And why in the world are you so interested in all this? Lord! I tell you that man is dangerous. He has a gun collection! And when he meets with his military staff you should hear what they talk about. I don't even want to know. Those things give me an awful feeling in the pit of my stomach. On Sundays, he takes the boy out early, says they're going to do some target practice. Can you believe it? Such a tiny little boy, with guns! That, to me, is a crime!"

It was all a crime, I thought to myself, starting with how they ended up with Miguel. Still, I was so happy. I had found him! I didn't know if I could do anything with the knowledge I had, but there was some comfort in knowing where he was. By the end of our conversation I had convinced Carmen to tell me if any jobs came open there. I knew there was only a remote possibility that this spoiled, pampered little boy would ever even speak a word to me or look in my direction, me, a servant—and an ex-convict! And I had a feeling all those security guards were to keep me from getting close to him at all. The guards were undoubtedly well informed. I would be risking everything if I even tried to see him.

Like Father . . .

Norma

Ricardo and Norma could never have imagined the joy this adopted son would bring to their lives. He wasn't just the thread that had mended the remnants of their failed marriage; he had become the backbone of the family. He was Ricardo's pride and joy. Now that Miguel was bigger, his father thoroughly enjoyed him, his games, his oversized imagination, and his insatiable curiosity. Ricardo knew his son idolized him. Miguel's admiration for his papá had no end; he wanted to be like him in every way and dreamed of following his footsteps into the military. He loved going to the barracks with his father, identifying ranks, badges, uniforms, and especially weapons. The colonel had a weapon collection he displayed in a majestic glass case in the living room. He was very proud of it. He took great pleasure in training his son in the use and value of each one.

On weekends, they would go to Miguel's grandparents' ranch in Puerto Berrio. The trips filled Ricardo with hope, because he knew that one day soon this vast pastureland with more than five hundred head of grazing cattle would belong to him. And, of course, Miguel would inherit it in his turn. This didn't matter so much to Norma; she knew she was the only heir to her parents' entire estate, and she'd had whatever she wanted whenever she wanted it since birth. It never occurred to her that it might not always be that way. The ranch was not even remotely attractive. She didn't like being out in the country, and she found no joy in the place, or the heat, or the mosquitoes, or the harshness of rural life. She much preferred to stay home. Many a time she would pull out some social event as an excuse to stay and enjoy the comforts of home or the club, or go out with friends in peace. It was a relief not to have to deal with Ricardo's bad moods and boorishness.

Miguel, by contrast, loved to ride horseback with his papá through the pastures, learning about the crops, the livestock, the types of grass, and how to run the ranch. At that tender age, under his father's tutelage, he learned that a boss needs to be even-tempered to manage workers, and he should always be firm and authoritative with them.

"Don't let them get away with looking you in the eye when they answer. They must keep their heads bowed and say, 'Yes, sir.' If you let up even a little bit, they will turn on you, and these people, even if they seem so obedient right there in front of you, they can be your worst enemy," he would warn.

Ricardo showed his son what commanding superiority he would have had over the ranch hands on his own parents' finca, had it stayed in the family. He never talked about his past or the tragedy his family suffered during *la violencia*. Norma didn't know anything about this side of her husband; he'd only mentioned it once or twice in passing. But Ricardo knew that if it weren't for the tragedy on his parents' finca, he would now be a simple coffee farmer on a smallish piece of land that paled in comparison to the luxurious Alvarez hacienda. He fancied this land would be his soon. He also fancied his military star would soon rise. His name was already being tossed about for promotion to general.

The only thing weighing him down was the state of the country. Violence had increased since the government had enacted the extradition law for drug traffickers, especially in Medellín. The Medellín Cartel had the minister of justice assassinated, and then the government cracked down on drug traffickers. So the narcos decided to test the mettle of both the government and the people, through violent attacks all over the country. Bombs would go off anytime and anywhere, and people working in the judicial system were slaughtered daily. It was cool to get a job as a hit man. Hired assassins murdered anyone without batting an eye. Medellín, the city of eternal spring, known for the cheerful, entrepreneurial paisa personality, turned into a city of horror. Colonel Restrepo knew that when Antioquians had opted to pay off narco-traffickers so they would defend ranchers against the guerrillas, they'd opened the door to a worse threat. Pablo Escobar was king in Medellín, and he was expanding his reach throughout the country.

Meanwhile, the government of peace had become the administration of confusion. The guerrilla groups that had signed ceasefires were complaining that the government had broken its promises. And the armed forces didn't hesitate to ramp up the conflict with unauthorized military attacks and operations to prove the peace negotiations had failed. Military leaders hoped the situation would boil over, so they could justify taking over the country when the people were finally ready to admit that the "president of peace" was an utter failure.

Clearly, the generals had it in for the president; they'd made it impossible for him to keep the promises he'd made for peace. Military leaders had been pushing back against what they considered a serious affront: There had been a secret meeting between the president and M-19 leaders in Mexico. The minister of defense went on and on in an article in the style magazine *Revista Diners* about the dangers of a weak, cowardly government, detailing how the military could overthrow it. That would not be an easy feat in a country that prided itself on being the oldest democracy in South America, mostly surrounded by military dictatorships. Appearances were everything. The world must see Colombia as a democratic, Christian, just, equitable, and happy country. It was all a farce that no one believed, but no one was truly able to question it, either. Ricardo simply sat back and waited, convinced that, this time, fate would grant him what he'd always wanted: a high rank in the military so he could finally run this gullible country. After all, anything was possible with absolute power.

At the Little Cabin

Amparo

"My god, you are so incredibly gorgeous," Amparo whispered to Mono as she ran her hands over his powerfully built chest and then down to his waist, where they began to explore unfettered. He let her do as she would, entranced.

They had met that day at the cabin Mono's mamá owned, up at the top of the hill. The town was a powder keg, and the last few months it had been harder and harder to meet. He finally gathered up his courage to invite her to the little cabin. Amparo knew Mono's mamá because she led a women's co-op in San Juan; her own mother went to it. They did needlework and handicrafts to sell at village fairs. Mono's mamá, doña Tere, taught them all. Amparo went with her mamá to a meeting once, but thought it was boring and didn't go back. All they did was talk about the threats against their husbands and the plans they had to leave everything behind if things got any worse.

◎

I wanted to know what was up with Mono: why was he so secretive?

"Why are we always sneaking around?" I asked.

"Baby, it's just that I really care about you, and I don't want anyone to know. I want to have you all to myself."

"Oh, yeah? So okay. Let's see. Tell me, where do you really live? Why don't you ever come to my house? My papá doesn't bite. What's all the mystery?"

"Who's that guy you were dancing with at the San Juan festival?" was his counter.

"What? You mean you're jealous? I barely know him. He spends all his time at don Eusebio's store."

"And what's his name?"

"I don't know his name. They call him "Chacho," sometimes "Comandante.""

Mono's antennae shot up at the word "comandante," and he wanted more information.

"Commander of the military brigade?"

"How should I know?! I already told you he doesn't say a whole lot. He's so serious. The other day he came to meet with my papá."

"Was he alone, or did he come with others?"

"There were about three of them, and after they left, my papá looked really worried. That's all I know."

"What did they talk about?"

"I have no idea. Oh, enough! You're such a dope!" I sat up again and tried to turn his mind back to me with my caresses.

Mono knew he wasn't going to get anything more out of me. I didn't want to tell him any more, either. Why waste these rare, precious moments on gabbing? My hands were at work to turn him on again, and in the end his mind proved weaker than his flesh. He held me close as he slowly penetrated me. Our passion rose steadily, and intermittent waves of pleasure crashed over us until we gave in to our excitement and climaxed together. We drifted off to sleep entangled in one another's arms, forgetting everything else.

It was past ten o'clock when we woke up. I jumped up, panicked, and pulled on my jeans as fast as I could while I begged him to take me home. There was no justifiable reason for me to be getting home so late. My father was going to beat me to a pulp. We rushed out and headed to the town plaza. As we approached my house, we saw lights.

"My papá has a meeting. Oh, I hit the jackpot! He won't know I'm not home," I said, trying to calm my pounding heart.

Mono peeked through the window, curious to see who was there. We saw police officers in a heated debate with other men in uniform. Mono said the olive-green camouflage—and especially the wide-rimmed sombreros—was very suspicious. I got that he was really interested in this meeting, but if they saw us looking through the window, I was going to catch hell.

"Go! Get out of here already! If my papá sees you, he'll kill you. I'm going in the back door so they won't see me."

We blew each other a kiss, and that was our goodbye.

Mono backed away a few steps, but he was still watching, hidden in the thickets. I was surprised to see Comandante at this meeting, too. They were caught up in their argument, so my father didn't notice how late I was. Comandante, however, shot me a reproachful look. I zipped up to my room and set about recalling every instant I'd shared with Mono. What would Cristina say when I told her! She would ask if I had used protection—she was always so practical. But how could I? If I bought anything at the pharmacy, the whole town would know. I didn't care, and I wasn't going to get upset about that, anyway. Let the world end! Let them all kill each other! I fell asleep to sweet dreams, mesmerized by the burning sensation that lingered between my legs.

Fleeting Glimpse
Mariate

Julián blew in out of nowhere one Friday at dusk. General Command had given him a few days off to spend time with his family. Mariate welcomed him as always, the joy of her postponed desire infused with uncertainty about the future. They didn't talk about the past or the future. All they talked about was the M-19. He was obsessed with the M-19.

Julián said M-19 commanders were frustrated because the president wasn't following through with the peace accords; they felt betrayed. So they were going to send a powerful message, turn the tables on the government and protest its inability to keep its promises.

"What powerful message?" Mariate asked, while she pat-pat-patted into shape some *arepas de choclo*, his favorite cornmeal cake made with special Andean corn.

"Yes. Just think about it. This administration will end within a year. Presidential elections are just around the corner. If we don't set the conditions for peace now, we never will. So, we're planning a big operation, and it will force the negotiations to break through or fall apart. This is the last card we have to play to define the country's future."

"And what do you have to do with all that?"

"Well . . . they've chosen me to be part of the mission," he declared. He was a proud, committed militant who was ready to give his life for his ideals.

Julián had been training for a few months already. The members of the mission were so compartmentalized they didn't even know where, when, or with whom they were going to work. One week before the operation they would be taken to an undisclosed location to receive their orders, and from that point on they would be incommunicado. But now he had a few days to rest, and the important thing was to enjoy them with his family.

Julián couldn't help but marvel at how big and strong Gabriel was. His joy and pride spilled over; he knew his bloodline would live on through the plucky Antioquian genes in his little boy. He spent as much time as he could with him, finding out what he liked, playing with him, and teaching him all the things he'd dreamed of teaching him for so long.

"Remember, you have to be brave and tough. You need to take care of your mamá, no matter what. Got it? I might be far away, but I am always thinking of you and I am with you in spirit, fighting against injustice. Never let anyone or anything trample on your rights."

This abstract speech made no sense to a two-and-a-half-year-old. But the little one listened anyway, his attention fixed on this man who said he was his papi. Julián asked him to tuck those words away in his memory forever. Protect his mamá and fight against injustice. The little boy nodded, but didn't understand. Protect his mamá . . . from what? Fight against injustice?

"What's injustice?" he asked in his garbled speech.

"Injustice, m'ijo, is when the rich screw the rest of us. That is why there is a revolution, to make sure future generations have a better country."

◎

I was listening from the kitchen and popped in just then to cut off the conversation. It was out of place.

"Amor, let's go to the park; let's take a walk with Gabriel. It's a beautiful day out!"

The truth was, I had a special plan for that Sunday. It was a gorgeous sunny day; the sky was an intense blue and a warm breeze floated gently down from the mountains, enveloping Medellín. We walked along Oriental Avenue to the Poblado neighborhood. When we got there, I went up to the doorman by Los Guaduales and asked him to call the maid in the penthouse, Tower C. Carmen knew the plan and came down to the building foyer to whisper hurriedly that Miguel would be coming out in half an hour to go to a birthday party. We had become close friends. I had never told her who I was to Miguel—I didn't dare because I didn't want to put her in a tough predicament. But she had clearly figured it out, and she was willing to facilitate this meeting with the tacit understanding that I wouldn't try anything.

And that is how it happened. Julián and I watched the armored military vehicle come out a bit later, with two guards up front and a boy of about six in the back. I was so excited to see the car park at the entrance while the driver got out to drop off some packages. The back window was open, so I could make out my muchacho's face. His hair was darker than what I remembered, and it was curly now. He had a serious, cocky look on his face that made him seem older than his scant six years. But it was Miguel. No doubt about it. It was him. Just then he looked out the window nonchalantly. He and Julián exchanged looks. Then he looked down at Gabriel, one of his hands clasped in mine and the other in his papi's, and finally he looked at me. I only had it in me to muster a smile that was both sweet and sad. It must have been confusing. Then he turned around, uninterested, and tried to hide in the seat. By the time the driver got in and the car was on its way, he had already forgotten us.

We didn't say a word on the way back. Julián must have felt guilty for not having kept his promise. And it must have been hard when he understood the long road I had traveled for such a tiny reward: the indifferent gaze of a little boy in the midst of a world we could never enter. Locking eyes with that little guy who belonged to a totally different universe left me with a bittersweet taste in my mouth. How could he know the power of our sacred bond of blood with just one look? It was confirmed once again that there was no way I'd get Miguel back.

It was Gabriel who broke the silence after a while, as he pulled on us to play with him, chattering as two-year-olds do. Finally, Julián forgot that he was the guerrillero fighting the system to protest injustice in his country. That day he was a father, a husband, and a lover, just like any other man in the park or at home on a Sunday, spending time with his family. That night he made love to me with more passion than either one of us could remember, in any of the few intimate moments life had granted us. The next morning I woke up, and the right side of our bed was empty. The only thing left was the scent of him, clinging to the sheets. I stretched out and buried my head in his pillow, hoping to steep in the essence of my man and imprint it on my brain forever. I knew I wouldn't see him again.

Don Eusebio

Amparo

"They killed don Eusebio! They killed don Eusebio!"

It was dawn. The news lashed at us like a whip. Don Eusebio's wife doña Celina ran to our house, pleading for justice. My papá, as the police chief, took charge, but deep down we all knew that there was nothing to be done.

"What happened?"

Her voice was broken by sobs as doña Celina recounted how the men in uniform had shown up in the wee hours of the morning. They barged in, shouting and threatening, pulled her husband out of bed, dragged him to the doorway, and summarily shot him three times—right there in front of his children.

"But why? You know don Eusebio never hurt anybody, he wasn't even involved in politics! He never took sides with any gangs," asked my mamá.

"They've been threatening us for a while. They told Eusebio to cut off supplies to the guerrillas. They said if they found out he was giving them even one grain of rice, they'd crush him. We tried to explain that we had no way of knowing who would end up with what people bought in his store. It was his little business. That's how we make a living."

Doña Celina was choking on her tears. She wiped her nose on her shawl, while my mamá tried to console her. Then she started talking again.

"On Monday, some muchachos came by, you know, as they always do, and they wanted camping supplies. My husband refused to sell them anything and fished for reasons why they wanted them. They demanded explanations, and he did his best to reason with them. Then they threatened to tear the store apart if they found out he was with the paracos. We were between a rock and a hard place."

"We all are, doña Celina," my papá said.

71

Other villagers started to show up, milling about, frightened and confused.

"I told Eusebio that we had to get out of here. He wouldn't listen; he was stubborn. He said he wasn't going to move off his land, it was all we had. We're old, and what would we live on if we went to the city? He hadn't done anything to hurt anyone. Why would anyone hurt him? That's what he said! And now look. Now what are we going to do? My kids are devastated. Our oldest already announced he's joining the guerrillas to get revenge for his father's death."

The neighbors were talking, and the rumor mill started. "It was Mayor Mariano's fault," they said. "He's turning in everyone he doesn't like. He thinks that's going to get him in good with them. He doesn't know they have him in their sights, too." Others added, "They're threatening the teachers, too, and people working at the Banco Agrario."

Just then Mono's mother came by. My mamá and doña Celina latched on to her as if she were a life preserver.

"What are we going to do, doña Tere? Where are we going to end up?" they cried.

"It was that Chacho guy again, wasn't it?" she asked. People started clamoring that they should all hightail it out of there.

Doña Tere warned: "No leaving houses or land. This town is our home, and we're not going to hand it over to these thugs. Go back to your work. We will honor don Eusebio as we should, as he is due, and we will have his funeral and bury him."

Everyone was muted, but they carried out her orders. That very night Padre Leandro held don Eusebio's funeral Mass, and later there was a candlelight vigil with friends and family walking through the village.

We didn't open the juice stand that day. Or in the days to come, for that matter. Chacho and his men were careful not to show their faces that week. I knew where they camped, and I thought it might be time now to have that date with the mystery man.

The House of Serenity

Norma

Madre Susana had disappeared from our lives after the whole adoption inci-
dent. Ricardo refused to talk to her, but I felt the poor woman deserved at
least some consideration. One weekend, when my husband and Miguel were at
the ranch, I decided to pay her a courtesy call in her new residence, the House
of Serenity.

After a tortuous ride over a narrow road up the mountain, I finally saw the
cloisters nestled in the hills at the edges of the town of La Ceja. At one time, it
had been a monastery. It was majestic. Now it belonged to the community; its
mission was to give nuns some well-deserved rest in their old age.

It was like a trip back into the Middle Ages. The solid, heavy walls of the
building evoked a life of introspection. The nun may well have needed it. She
seemed surprised to see me, and she was not particularly happy or welcoming.
She led me through the halls of the cloisters and introduced me to some of the
other sisters who lived there.

The sisters spent the better part of their days in prayer and domestic work
like sewing, embroidering, or tending the garden, to pass the time. She didn't
pray, though. I didn't ask, but she explained she had never been inclined to pray
the way her religious life required.

"For me religion is like politics—both are a farce invented by the powers
that be to maintain their power over the weak."

"So why did you become a nun, Madre?"

The time she'd spent in this asylum seemed to have made her more talkative,
because that day her heart was an open book.

"Look, Norma, I did not enter the religious order by choice. It was my fate.
The only alternative I had at a crucial point in my life."

Life in the country and the mountains rising majestically beyond the plateau reminded her of her childhood on her parents' hacienda. Like good Antioquians, her grandparents' generation had cleared the sides of the central mountain range so they could have small but productive mountain-zone plantations, like coffee and banana. Her grandparents had been coffee growers, as had her parents, and as she and her brother would have been, if their fates had not steered them down a different path.

She couldn't remember exactly when it was that happiness began to fade. She did remember the cracks beginning to appear in her blissful girlhood when she was on the cusp of adolescence and the political spats in the area intensified. The Conservatives in power under Laureano Gómez's administration had hired assassins called *pájaros* to annihilate the Liberals.

It was a startling level of violence that caused hordes of displaced people to seek refuge in the mountains. And that was how bands of savage killers, out for revenge, were born. They were the *bandoleros* who harassed both city and country folk. Her parents were Liberals through and through, but they tried to keep their distance from the conflict. They only wanted to live in peace and raise their children in a healthy environment.

That was also when she met her first love. She recounted wistfully how she met Alfonso one Sunday after Mass. Then she saw him again at a traditional festival in the area; he took advantage of the hullabaloo to give a white lily to her, "the loveliest flower at the carnival."

Driven by adolescence's insatiable passion, it didn't take long for Susana and Alfonso to fall in love. They would meet every Sunday after Mass, or at fiestas where girls could talk to boys without raising eyebrows. When Susana gathered up the courage to ask her father if she could invite her suitor over, he issued a categorical no and stood firm on the incontestable argument of political affiliations.

"M'ija, don't you understand what it means that he's a Conservative? He's an Uribe, the grandson of that damned *chulo* thug who terrorizes everyone with his threats!"

"Papá, that is no reason to say I can't have a boyfriend. It's not his fault we are from families with different political ideas, and it's not mine. What does it matter, anyway? We don't care."

"Well, it matters, hija, and you better listen to your parents; you don't second-guess us. I absolutely forbid it. I don't have to give you any explanation, but I did. When you're older, you'll understand that in this country, things like this are really important."

They were, indeed. Susana would soon learn the painful, bloody lesson that spats pitting Liberal versus Conservative were motive enough to tap the deep-seated hatred passed down from generation to generation. Alfonso and Susana were not swayed by their parents' prohibitions. They just took their love into hiding. They would meet after school and run for the cover of the solitary coffee trees covering the Antioquian hills. They were free without parental supervision and soon discovered the pleasure their bodies could provide. They made love with the innocent eagerness of their sixteen years.

This was the happiest time of her life, and Susana held nothing back as she recalled it. It was as if, by talking about it, the door to her iron heart would swing open. Her joy, however, was short-lived. It wasn't long before their parents found out about their secret encounters, and punishment was as swift as it was brutal. Susana was locked up in the hacienda; she couldn't even leave to go to Mass.

She was kept in isolation. A spinster aunt, *tía* Berta, lived with them and took charge of watching her, making sure she had no contact with the outside world. Tía Berta brought her food three times a day. She could go out once a day to walk around the ranch. But never alone. Susana stoically resigned herself to her fate. She did not complain even once and made certain no one ever saw her cry. Still, the result of her rendezvous under the coffee trees was soon visible. Her aunt figured it out when Susana would not eat. She wasn't trying to be difficult; she truly was nauseous. Tía Berta told Susana's parents immediately. It was the worst family scandal ever.

At that time, there was no fate more horrible for a woman than being a single mother. It stained her whole family by extension, and it was a particularly black spot on the man's honor. A traditional, deeply Christian family would separate the disgraced woman from the rest of the family. That was what Susana feared. But she was wrong. Her father was categorical.

"Things like this never remain under wraps for long, and there's even more gossip if you hide a daughter away. This child is a curse and should not be born."

Her mother and tía Berta were scandalized and adamantly opposed to an abortion. It was against Christian teachings. But he had made up his mind.

He appeared one night with a village midwife, and she took care of it. Susana didn't even have time to fully comprehend what was happening. She was taken to a dark room and drugged with something awfully bitter. Then they performed a rudimentary procedure on her. They botched the operation so horribly that she nearly bled to death.

Her mother complained to her husband: "Why take all your anger out on her and not on the scum who dishonored her? Or are you not man enough to make him pay for your daughter's honor?"

"A dishonored daughter is worthless," was his retort. Yet he conceded his wife was right.

One night after a drinking binge at a village bar, her father ran into Alfonso and laid into him. That in turn ignited the fury of the muchacho's family. The next day a whole retinue showed up to settle accounts with don Elias Restrepo. He was ready, and before they could cross the gate into his finca he ran them off with his musket.

"Damned Conservative *Godos*, get off my land! Get outta here!" and he and his hired hands ran the Uribe party off with gunshots blazing.

Retribution was swift. Early one morning Susana heard the thunder of horses' hooves. She had been sleeping in a room set off from the rest of the house with tía Berta since her punishment began. She could see from her window the posse closing in on the main house, the men wielding fiery torches. She watched the house as it went up in flames after they'd doused the straw roof with gasoline. Shrieks; howls; curses. Horror. She managed to alert her brother Ricardo, whose room was closest to hers. She ordered him to run and not look back.

The three escaped to the mountains. Susana was still weak from her operation and struggled to keep up as they fled. Ricardo took her under the arm, and then carried her when she fainted. That was how they stumbled into the closest village and found refuge at a friend's house. The Uribes set up checkpoints all around the area, so they could not get back home. They couldn't even give their family a Christian burial. Their parents and four little brothers perished that night.

She had left everything buried deep in the past, including the horror of that fateful night. The finca would later be occupied by some of the countless cheats who profited from the violence by taking over land and turning it into coffee empires. She and her brother would never be able to go back.

Her tía was old and ailing. She barely had the wherewithal to get Susana to the Dominican convent, because it accepted any young girl as a postulant, no questions asked. Ricardo's situation wasn't so cut and dried. She had to call on favors from relatives who had connections with the military, and then use what little savings she had to pay his tuition at Bogotá's military school, the Escuela Militar de Cadetes. Ricardo just met the age requirement for enrollment. And both resigned themselves to their fates.

"What ever happened to your tía?" I asked. I was curious, since my husband had never mentioned any other relative.

They never saw tía Berta again. They didn't know if she had died or if she had just decided to forget the past. Both had been registered as orphans, and from that point on, they were at the mercy of institutions.

I was surprised the nun had set aside her arrogance and very pleased to finally uncover part of my husband's history. I had never been able to draw anything out of him about his past, even after so many years of marriage.

We were on the monastery terrace overlooking the vast plains rolling out beneath us when Madre Susana finished. I spied a tear that had evaporated on her glasses. Somehow, by dusting off the files of her past, she could see herself more objectively: She was a woman with no choice. If she hadn't joined the nunnery, she would've been a streetwalker. That was her choice. She harbored no more hopes for her life. She saw her fate as one more loop in a repetitive cycle. The violence that had taken the lives of her family expanded as it spun out into a dizzying spiral.

But there was something that she could not make peace with, and that was the loss of her unborn baby. She confessed that no one knew that—not even Ricardo. Then she cloaked herself in deep silence. It dawned on me that she was having this crisis of conscience because she had repeated that very cycle with an innocent woman, just to make me and Ricardo feel better. And yet, in the whole conversation that afternoon, she never once mentioned Miguel or where he came from. It was a sacred secret for both of us, hanging over our heads like the blade of a guillotine. And it would remain buried deep in the coffers of our unspeakable secrets.

The Visit

Mariate

"Nora! Hermana, my sister, this is a miracle! How did you find me?"

"Come on, you know we ELNers don't have secrets! And you're still one of us."

Nora had come with a mission: to bring Mariate into the ranks of the ELN. She explained that the command knew all about her and her time in prison. And her training.

◎

"We need people like you," said Nora, "people who are strong and committed and true to their word. This is a crucial time in our political history. The government wasn't following through, the military kept attacking the M-19, so finally the M-19 had to completely break the truce. That's why we ELNers won't make any deals. I told you in prison, the time just isn't ripe yet. We are pulling together a contingency front to push for peace with social justice, as Camilo Torres said. Do you remember our debates?"

I was comfortable with Nora; she was my friend and compañera, and had shared so much with me in prison. But that was years ago, and my priority now was to make a good future for Gabriel.

"You wouldn't take me with a two-year-old. Besides, now we know where Miguel is. Julián and I want to keep track of him, just in case . . ."

"In case what? You know you'll never get him back. How are you going to stand up to an army colonel and all the power behind him? You, all on your little ol' lonesome? Join us, and we will help you. We could plan an operation to get Miguel and tell him the truth. We were there; we saw them steal him from you," said Nora matter-of-factly.

"It is not okay to play with a child's life like that," I replied laconically. I'd heard all of it before: promises to plan a guerrilla operation to get Miguel back. It wouldn't happen. No guerrilla group would go up against a soldier in the army for something so personal. Not for nothing in return.

◉

So Mariate didn't take Nora up on her offer, but she was so happy to see her again. It felt good not to feel so alone and to know that she could count on her friend's help if she ever needed it.

Nora was still happy-go-lucky and self-assured, but now she was a high-ranking commander in the ELN front stationed around El Retiro. She had a son, too, with her compañero, Iván; but as so often happened in situations like hers, she had left her child with her family.

◉

"Paisa, please try to see where I'm coming from. I don't need to get messed up in anything. My needlework business is doing well. I even have a few ware-houses buying from me and some textile companies sending me orders. I don't even need to clean houses anymore. I live a peaceful life, and that's the way I want to keep it. I'm still not ready to give up my second child." And with that, I left Nora with no more arguments.

"I understand, Hermana. You know that if you ever change your mind, we will welcome you with open arms. Your country needs you!"

◉

Nora's visit deeply unnerved Mariate, especially now when she was waiting anxiously for a call, a letter—any sign of life—from Julián. She was used to long silences, but this time she had a terrible feeling in her gut. She was so worried that the only thing that calmed her down was knitting. It was her emotional refuge: knit, purl, knit, purl, knit. The art of interlacing colors together to create her own patterns, freehand, was a balm on her loneliness. It was her therapy. That was how she spent the hours when sleep evaded her, and that—these days—was the case more often than not. She never went anywhere without her tuft of wool, knitting, pulling it out, knitting it over again, never saying a word. And she waited. And waited. Even Gabriel's goofiness couldn't distract her anymore. Her intuition gnawed at her, deep down in her soul. Worry hung over her head like the sword of Damocles.

Dread

Amparo

A silence more terrifying than the days of thunder that had come before it descended on the village.

The death of don Eusebio cut the entire village to the core. School closed for a week; the Banco Agrario only opened two hours a day; the health clinic was open, but there weren't any doctors anymore. Father Leonardo would rush in on Sundays, say a hurried Mass, and make tracks out of town right after.

Lots of our neighbors were packing up and trying unsuccessfully to sell off the few remaining things they had. Farms built up and run for years with back-breaking work were abandoned overnight. Acres and acres of corn, left to wither in the sun. Fruit splattered onto the ground and rotted. Skeletal animals were wandering around aimlessly, or strewn here and there on the road. Dead. Pastures were blanketed in weeds, and everyone was desperately anxious.

My mamá begged my papá to resign as chief—to go anywhere but there. "Let's go back to Sabaneta, m'ijo," she pleaded constantly. "At least there's a future there. What is there for our kids here?" All he could do was hold his head in his hands. There was nothing to say.

◎

Chacho and his men did not show their faces in the village again. Any loyal officers who were left were standing guard with don Luciano. Anything could happen. Amparo was always on the alert now; she'd listen through the walls to conversations between her father and his officers. Did Chacho leave? That was the big question. The answer was no; he had not finished his mission. So where were they holing up? Some were saying they were camped out by the cemetery, on top of the rocky hill. What were they planning up there? What were they waiting for? And the guerrillas? They were still there, prepping and waiting for reinforcements, they said.

◎

And what about us? We radioed for help to the brigade and the police, and sent requests to the government for more support. But we got nothing. The brigade said they couldn't justify sending in troops for a few reports of skirmishes. "What if later is too late?" my papá demanded. Clearly, we didn't really matter.

Meanwhile, I hid in my favorite place: my room. I passed the time dreaming of when I was in Mono's arms. I was waiting with bated breath for a call, a message. But nothing. Not one word since that night.

Where was Chacho? The one who had all of San Juan under his thumb? For some odd reason, he didn't intimidate me. Not at all. In fact, I bet that if I talked to him, he might listen to me and leave us alone. Why not? If I could work my charms on him—and there was no doubt about that—maybe we could talk some sense into him. But how? If only I could get close enough to him to talk.

It was a great idea. I could wrap him around my little finger. I knew I could. The idea that I could save the entire village began to take shape in my mind. It was already clear, and becoming clearer all the time.

The Siege
Mariate

Mariate found out she was pregnant again the very day that Julián died. She knew that he was gone from the moment every station on the radio started reporting that the M-19 had stormed the Palacio de Justicia. That was the big mission Julián had been preparing for.

It was all over the radio.

An M-19 commando of thirty-five guerrilleros took over the Supreme Court building right in front of the Capitol building, just a block away from the presidential residence, Nariño Palace, in Bogotá. They called it the "Antonio Nariño Operation for Human Rights." All the judges, staff, and administrative personnel who happened to be in the building were taken hostage. The M-19 got in, set up, and then called the news stations. They were calling out the president for not keeping the peace accords, and denouncing the government's violations of the truce.

Retribution was swift. The Thirteenth Brigade sent land and air troops in for the counter-offensive. Orutú and Cascavel armored war tanks rolled into Plaza de Bolívar and started to fire. Everything was televised live. It was like a Hollywood action flick: attacks coming from all sides, helicopters hovering over Special Operations Police commandos, machine guns and torpedoes blasting all around the Palacio de Justicia. The war tanks were the scariest. They were state-of-the-art armored tanks, but they looked like relics from the past. Every blast shook the earth as absurdly large bombs tore apart the building's walls. It was a macabre spectacle.

It was covered live, 24/7. Everyone heard the chief justice and his heart-rending pleas:

"*Por favor*, hold your fire! You're killing us; you are killing the hostages! Please, Mr. President, say something! Order them to stop the attack!"

The pleas became more and more harrowing as time wore on and there was still no response from the head of state. Dusk fell, and the silence was deafening. All of Colombia was demanding to know how in the world the commander in chief could refuse to answer. This was the same head of state who had promised "not one more drop of blood." The one who'd chanted "Yes, we can" during his campaign and all three years of his presidency. He was being considered for the Nobel Peace Prize. It made no sense. The archbishop of Bogotá offered to mediate, and the chairman of the Episcopal Commission pleaded for an end to the barrage, but not even that could mitigate the brutality of the attack. The reporters could not believe it. The magistrates were dumbfounded. The entire country spiraled down into a state of chaos.

The President Is President No More
Norma

Colonel Restrepo called Norma that afternoon from the army headquarters in Medellín. His voice belied his excitement as he relayed what had happened. When his wife asked him why the head of state was not responding to the pleas of the chief justice, Ricardo responded joyfully:

"Don't be naive, amor. The president is president no more, and he has no say in what is going on. General Vega Uribe and Colonel Plazas are in charge now. It is high time we stopped clowning around with peace talks and amnesties. Now we are the ones in charge of where the country is headed."

"But what about the hostages and the Supreme Court justices?"

"The judges and the hostages? Let them figure it out. Collateral damage. We'll build statues to them," said Ricardo.

In truth, the interoffice memo sent when the attack began had foretold everything: "All military brigade commandos: high alert. Regiments stand ready." General Vega Uribe (the minister of defense) and General Samudio led the offensive. Their orders were to liquidate the revolutionaries. The high command of the armed forces met in the president's own office to plan the relentless attack. There was no mercy. They ordered their forces to finish off the terrorists and show no pity. They should leave absolutely no room for mediation. Shoot anything that moved. It was the perfect storm they had been waiting for to make the president pay for everything: for being weak, for reducing the expanded powers of the armed forces, for cutting their budgets. The perfect time to teach the guerrillas a lesson and make them forget their bogus aspirations and good intentions. Dialogue? Negotiations? What they were going to get was lead. The generals were not going to repeat the humiliation they had endured five years ago when the guerrillas took over the embassy of the Dominican Republic. They had not forgotten the utter humiliation of that fiasco. This was how the military would prove who had real power and authority.

Night fell. The Palacio de Justicia was shot through like a pincushion. The gasses from the explosives mixed, and the Palacio began to burn. The fire soon licked throughout the building's many wings. The guerrillas freed some hostages, but as soon as they stepped out of the door, most were gunned down by the army. The scene was captured on camera for the whole country to behold: the building consumed by the inferno, flames shooting up into a sulfur sky.

Is Julián There?

Mariate

It was ghastly. I couldn't take it anymore. The TV was trained on the Palacio de Justicia, which was buckling under the flames. The media had lost all contact with the guerrilleros and the hostages. I had identified who the leaders of the operation were at the beginning of the attack: Julián's compañeros Luis Otero, El Negro Jacquín, and others he admired fiercely. I could feel the life of my man go out behind the furious blaze. And my fate was sealed.

I held Gabriel against my chest and whispered: "M'ijito, we're on our own now; it's just you and me."

My sister overheard me and whirled around to face me.

"Is Julián there? He's in a guerrilla commando? No, oh, no, not that! Do *not* get me involved in that. Now they're going to come and ransack everything. I am not going to risk my life or the lives of my children for your husband's stupid dreams and his terrorist friends!"

"Take it easy, Jacinta. I don't know if he's there; it's just a feeling I have. Forget it; I'm just really sensitive these days."

Deep down I wanted to hope that it might not be true, that Julián would be one of the guerrilleros who had survived an attack a few weeks earlier in Cali. The early hours of Thursday morning found me with my ear to the radio and my eyes on the TV, holding tight to my single strand of hope. Everything they said that day was a jumble of contradictions. They were saying it looked like some people might have survived in a bathroom that didn't burn down. But the chief justice had fallen silent. The media could only speculate about what was going on inside and about what was clearly unforgivable: the silence of the president.

Bloodbath
Norma

By noon on Thursday it was all over. The president did not break his silence. Not even at the very end, when the media were blaring out the numbers of dead and wounded brought out through the front door. Not even when they counted the judges and the entire judicial branch and all the guerrilleros.

Then something very odd happened. The military pulled out. It was as if its mission to liquidate the revolutionaries had been completed, but when they understood the magnitude of the tragedy they'd perpetrated, they skulked away. They were triumphant, winning their power, and then it turned on them. They would never be able to justify such a gruesome bloodbath. The chief justice died pleading with them to stop the assault. He was suffocated by all the gasses and the thick smoke inside the inferno. When the press interviewed those few survivors, they condemned the counterattack. "The guerrilleros were not attacking us. They were defending us, protecting us from the military attacks!" The few guerrilleros who got out alive were taken to the Casa del Florero by Plaza de Bolívar and interrogated. Then they disappeared to the Caballerizas torture camp. Most of the low-level staff, students, and interns who were at the Palacio and died that day were labeled "subversives" on their death certificates. Others were just never seen again.

The country felt utterly powerless. No one could figure out what had happened. And no one was coming forward or offering any explanation. Journalists tried to find military officials, but they had mysteriously disappeared. The generals and other officials couldn't justify their actions to the nation, and so they ended up vacating the president's office.

And the president was found by a Palacio de Nariño press office journalist, locked up in the Council of Ministers' room with some of his closest aides.

They were all terrified and completely in the dark about what had happened. The head of state had no idea what had just shaken all of Colombia to its core, but he was flung nonetheless at the helm again and had to answer to the country for the biggest massacre in its history. And that is what he did. He gave his speech that night on TV. His face was wan and he looked unsteady, but he had the courage to say: "I am responsible for what happened. It is impossible to have dialogue with this breed of violence."

Just one day before, my husband, Colonel Restrepo, had been so arrogant, so drunk with power. Now he was hermetically silent. He tried to brush me off when I asked how the president would have to claim responsibility for what had happened when actually he had had nothing to do with it. He tried to convince me that the military had not ever taken over. It was me, I had interpreted it all wrong. When I wouldn't let up, he threatened me: "Norma, get this straight. You are a liar, and you had better think twice before you repeat it to anyone. *Ever!* You got that?"

I pretended I didn't understand a thing, but that was the moment when many truths were unveiled to me. I finally realized that we were living a farce: The state was vulnerable, and our democracy was a joke. I had until that moment chosen not to see or understand, and that day as I faced the significance of what had just happened, my eyes were opened to a dramatically different reality. On that sixth of November, Colombia suffered one of the greatest tragedies in its history. It marked the end of a peace plan and the beginning of an era of unrelenting violence.

No Direction
Mariate

The next day the press released the identity of everyone who had died in the operation, including the thirty-five members of the M-19. I recognized the picture and the name of my husband, Julián Jaramillo Arango, alias Mono (1957–1985). The list of the dead guerrilleros was complete. That day I cried myself dry. I was steeped in bitterness, but I could not forgive him. Injustice? Let me give you injustice: Abandon us so you can go follow some unclear, fantastic, intangible cause. I couldn't forgive him for the situation he'd put me in, either. Now what little I had fought so hard for would be taken from me. Military reprisal against anyone related to "terrorists" was merciless. I didn't even have the luxury of mourning over him. I had to get out of there fast, or my son and I would not be safe. My sister Jacinta shouted over and over, overcome by panic:

"Get out of my house! I don't want to have anything to do with this! They're going to come! They're going to turn this house upside-down and it's your fault. You fool! Why in the world did you hook up with a guerrillero? I told you, María Teresa. Get out of here!"

From then on, I knew I would build a new life. There would be no tears, no pain, no sorrow or regrets. I had myself, and I was going to fight against the system that had ripped my first son from me and had now killed my man. I swore that was the last it would take from me. I had two sons left, Gabriel Angel and the one who was just now growing in my belly.

I threw a few things in a backpack and pulled a ruana over my head. I grabbed Gabriel by the hand, and without saying a single word, we left my sister's house. We said no goodbyes. We were not headed in any particular direction. Where was I going to go? Somewhere, I guess. I knew then that my next baby would be a boy, too, and I was going to name him Rafael, after the archangel and patron saint of the traveler.

Part Two

I am the cosmic mother
who nursed you
with fire
only to
forsake you in a
promised land
where Being has a price.
Death.

—MARIA ISABEL GIRALDO

Where Was Miguel?

Norma

After her husband died, Norma withdrew more than she had ever imagined possible. The Los Guaduales penthouse had become her refuge and her sole consolation. It wasn't just because of her grief—her fear had turned into obsessive panic. She was afraid to go out, afraid to get in a car, and no matter how many bodyguards she had, she was afraid to take even a few steps out on the sidewalk. She felt hounded, like she was constantly under attack. She much preferred the fantasy of safety in her penthouse to the horror outside. In the penthouse, she was closer to the sky and the mountains.

Nevertheless, what upset her most was Miguel. It had been a while since Norma had known where he was. He had turned strangely inward since Ricardo's funeral. Despite his brilliant military career at such a young age, he left things from one day to the next. Left, without a word about where he was headed. Norma ignored the rumors swirling about her. His brigade buddies said he was probably in Córdoba. "A lot of guys leave the military to join up with fronts in that area. It makes sense; since the attorney general dictates what we can and can't do to stop the guerrillas, it's impossible to work here." Norma knew the rumors did not bode well for Miguel.

She pleaded with God: Make this go away. There was no way Miguel could turn into one of those whom she had always condemned and feared, even if a lot of people did support the paras regardless of where they came from. She spent her days lurching back and forth between depression and loneliness, agonizing over how to find Miguel. By that point her only companion was Carmen, who had stayed with her out of loyalty. Or maybe compassion. Or maybe just because she didn't have anywhere else to go.

"Señora, I brought you a little snack: arepa de choclo with cheese and coffee. Now don't you go and let it get cold. Look at yourself; you're just skin and bones."

The distance between servant and employer, so marked years ago, had dissipated over time. They had shared so much that at last friendship won out over social class. Carmen knew all her secrets. Even the ones that Norma herself didn't know she had.

Norma knew, after she lost everything, that her friends and the busy social life she had once enjoyed were gone. Many friends had fled the country out of fear; others left after they were threatened with kidnapping or retaliation. Those who had stayed were almost bankrupt like she was. Her relatives were going through the same thing; most had long since left the country. The rest forgot her completely when she lost her wealth, and she was marginalized socially. Carmen was the only one who stayed when misfortune befell the Alvarez family. Her job was now just to keep her boss alive, keep her from sinking deeper into depression. Norma depended on her for even her most intimate needs.

"Carmen, please bring me my sleeping pills and Xanax. That's all I want. And take this coffee away. I have no desire to drink it right now."

"Señora, the nun, the colonel's sister, called again. I almost didn't recognize her this time because now she goes by Susana, that's it."

"What did she say?"

"She asked again for you to call her. Call her, for the love of God."

"I don't get it. I haven't seen her since Ricardo died, and I thought she wanted to keep it that way."

I had caught sight of her, alone in a corner, at the funeral. We barely even exchanged condolences. Her interest in Miguel surprised me, though. She went to him and tried to talk, but he paid her no attention. She tried a few more times, until she finally understood that it was pointless. He was already in another world. His father was dead, and his own universe had collapsed. He loved his papá above all others; he was his rock, his guide. What could she want from me now? Money? She must know I was nearly broke. Deep down I knew the call was about something else. That was why I avoided it.

I got up out of my chair, went over to the picture window overlooking the balcony, and looked out over the whole of the Valle de Aburrá. I contemplated the majestic panorama the valleys and the mountains made, and wondered yet again where Miguel was. What he was up to. I thought about it for a few more seconds and then decided: I didn't really want to know after all.

The Co-op
Mariate

After don Eusebio's murder, Mariate's house became the refuge for many a San Juan villager. Civilian and military officials could not protect them, and the village and its inhabitants were left to fend for themselves in a sea of chaos. In a way, Mariate had become the anchor that everyone needed so badly.

They used the San Juan Craft Co-op Mariate had launched a couple of years ago as cover for their meetings. Women of all ages and backgrounds—from the police chief's wife to area peasants—were already members, and their industrious hands crafted the handiwork they made together at the tiny cabin. Some had been in San Juan for ages, but others had come recently, after being displaced from neighboring villages. Many were now heads of broken homes, taking on all responsibility for their small children and trying to build some stability.

Slowly, over time, the women had begun to realize how much power they had as heads of households, especially after their men were forced to join armed groups or flee if they didn't want to be killed. Now the group had become more political, and their chats centered on how to survive, with all the danger they had to navigate in the region. That afternoon they were talking about don Eusebio's murder. His widow doña Celina was a member of the co-op, too. That brutal atrocity was the last straw. It marked the moment when they decided they were going to determine how they could defend themselves against the constant attacks from both sides fighting for control of the village: the guerrillas, on the one hand, and the auto-defensas, on the other.

◎

While her hands spun thread, her fingers nimbly working the fibers, the police chief's wife doña Rosa filled them in on some interesting developments. "I just heard about some groups called Peace Communities; most area mayors have joined. They are neutral; they flatly refuse to take sides. What I don't get is why our own mayor isn't joining in."

"He doesn't think it's in his best interest. All he wants is to get on the good side of whoever he thinks will benefit him the most. That's why he's going around pointing fingers at villagers he doesn't like," replied doña Celina. She was understandably bitter, given recent events, but her voice rang out clearly, and she didn't miss a stitch as her sewing machine whirred on.

"Maybe. Or maybe he just doesn't have a choice," I piped up.

"You think so, doña Tere?" several women looked up, questioning as they worked.

"We don't always choose our fates," I said, disillusioned. But I went on. "I've learned after a whole lot of running that we can't outrun our destinies. They follow us wherever we go."

"And what've you been running from?" asked doña Celina.

"Ah, doña Celina, it's such a long story. If you only knew; it's just not worth the trouble."

Doña Celina pressed so hard for me to uncover my mysterious past that she convinced me the time had come to reveal it.

"Well, all right. Here it is. The guerrillas are at the root of all my problems, and the guerrillas were also my only hope when I fled my sister's house the day my husband died."

Everyone at the co-op stopped working and circled around me. They all wanted to know more.

"The ELN welcomed me with open arms when I finally managed to find them, using the clues Nora—my friend from Buen Pastor—had given me. I joined the Antioquian Northeast Front and became a fierce guerrillera. I was tough and resolute. I had left compassion and sentimentalism behind. Before long, I rose in the ranks, and took on important positions in the ELN command.

"My third son, Rafael, was born in a guerrilla camp. He was a breech baby, and it was a very difficult birth. They went to the closest hamlet and brought up a midwife to help me, but even her skill couldn't get him to turn. I was ready to give up when one of the commanders, who had some medical background, took over. He turned him, and Rafael was born, all gray from lack of oxygen. But he made it, thanks to the love and care my compañeros and I gave him. Sometimes I think it'd have been a greater salvation to have spared him this world altogether, considering the shaky future in store for him.

"Straightaway, the baby was a problem; the high command told me I couldn't keep him with me anymore. So, I was face to face with one of the most difficult dilemmas in my life. If I went back to the city, I would be risking arrest, and this time my record as a subversive was well documented—I was in the system, and the intelligence agency and national police knew who I was. Plus, after the horror of the Palacio de Justicia, the government had launched an all-out witch hunt to rout out M-19 members, their relatives, and supporters. A blanket of silence had been cast over the bloody event, and no one dared lift it for fear of what still lurked under it. Everyone knew that innocent people had been tortured by the army as it scrambled to mete out punishment for the massacre. Years would pass before charges would be brought and the guilty would be named in the wake of the Palacio massacre. It never crossed the minds of the M-19 command that by seeking justice, they would set in motion so much more injustice."

"Doña Tere, then what happened?" the ladies asked curiously.

"Leaving the guerrillas was not an option. The ELN had welcomed me enthusiastically, but it showed deserters no mercy. I was forced to leave my baby with my sister in Medellín. Yes. My sister Jacinta. The same sister who had kicked me out of her house. And she had no choice but to take my baby in. One more little one, among the many she already had to take care of. She didn't do it out of concern or compassion. He was just another rug rat raised by the grace of God, or better yet, raised Godless and lawless. I hoped that at least Rafael would grow up in a better place with Jacinta, but that didn't happen. I tried to see him whenever I could sneak into the city, and he knew who his mother was. But we didn't bond the way mother and child should. He wasn't even ten when my sister told me he had joined a gang in a Medellín district. That was when Pablo Escobar was recruiting kids from the communes for his band of killers.

"They allowed Gabriel to stay with me because he was older. Soon he started training in the art of war. He inherited his father's nickname 'Mono,' and he was proud to carry on the legend of his father's courage and strength. He was all I had left of Julián, all I had as consolation. All I had to honor his memory.

"That was how nearly twenty years went by, and there were truces and confrontations, administrations of peace and administrations of war. There never was even one resolution that could justify so much pain. The word 'peace' has turned into one of the main reasons to keep the war going. The auto-defensas were formed to fight the guerrillas, but they turned out to be more ruthless than the guerrillas! By that point, the M-19 was no longer an armed group.

Their last commander, Carlos Pizarro, signed peace accords with the government; they traded their guns in for the right to form the political party Alianza Democrática, the Democratic Alliance. Now some who had led the M-19 were in Congress, some had even run for the presidency. But as for Pizarro, he was assassinated shortly after he signed the amnesty and turned over his weapons; he never got to see the peace he wanted so badly.

"No one believed in peace processes anyway. For decades administration after administration had signed accord after accord and truce after truce; every single one had been blocked and had morphed into a new dispute and a new offensive. Remember our most recent peace process? The government demilitarized acres of land in the south and then handed it over to the FARC. The result was a general outcry that gave way to new and bloodier confrontations. The state has been so very weak that paramilitary groups thrive, and people support them because they think they will wipe out the guerrillas. There've been so many corrupt, weak presidents that the whole of Colombia is pleading for a strong leader. A firm hand. Someone to put an end to the agony.

"When I turned thirty-five, I asked to be discharged from the ELN. I decided to take refuge in San Juan, where I could do what I really liked: knitting, needlework, and weaving. A nice nun had taught me how to knit and embroider when I had my first baby in prison. They stole him from me, and the only thing I had left was needlework. Later I perfected what little I knew by taking some classes at SENA. That was what I did before I joined the ELN, but even when I was in the guerrilla, I sewed whenever I could get my hands on needles and thread. Knitting and spinning became my spiritual balm, they were all that could calm the guilt rumbling inside me. They have continued to keep me going, and now they keep the whole co-op going. We use what we make here to support our families. At least no one can take that away from us."

Hushed expectancy fell over her audience as Mariate's story sank in. Doña Celina was the first to break the silence.

"You've lost three sons in the treadmill of war."

"And my husband, too."

"How long have we been at this? Fighting this invisible enemy?" asked doña Celina.

"And those of us who still have men here, we know they don't have much time left," pointed out doña Rosa. "When will it stop?"

The women looked around in silence, their hands still busy sewing and weaving together their fading hopes and dreams. One over the other, the threads crisscrossed and wove together, combining colors and shapes on the warp stretched taut over the looms. The figures and textures gained in clarity with each pass through. Their hands alternated thread and heddle with the skill that only comes with experience. Each woman at her station, adding her own special touch through spinning, design, the pattern, or the composition. The looms beat out a rhythm as they spun and wove. It synchronized their thoughts into one, single, deliberately restrained demand for answers.

The cabin was hot and stuffy. Mariate paused for a moment to look at her compañeras. All at once she was struck by the plain truth right in front of her. They were the key to their own power. They were the best weapon against war, precisely because they had survived their men.

Into the Lion's Den

Amparo

spent the whole day mulling over an idea that had been taking shape in my head for days. That is how I spent math class, history, religion, and Spanish. I didn't say anything to anyone, not even Cristina, and I told her everything— absolutely everything. I had gone over every single detail. My mother was at the Tuesday co-op meeting, and as always, she had hired someone to work at the stand. She wouldn't know I was gone until that night. My father was at the police station and wouldn't be back with the family until very late, and my brother would be out with his friends. He wouldn't be all that worried about where I was. He would figure I had gone to a movie, or just gone out.

I got out of school at one in the afternoon. I didn't go downtown the way I usually did. I didn't go to the juice stand, either. I didn't wait for Cristina or any of my compañeras who almost always went out with me, giggling and gossiping as teenage girls do.

I headed in an entirely different direction, toward the cemetery. No one ever hung around there, especially now. My legs trembled more and more with every step; I had a vague, floating sensation lurching between terror and anxiety. There was still time to turn back, but something stronger pushed me on. There was no going back. It was something I was destined to do; a supernatural power propelled me on, and I offered it no resistance. I was fully aware that I was heading right into the lion's den, but I kept walking that path anyway, cocksure of what I was doing.

The Secret

Norma

Madre Susana had been diagnosed with pancreatic cancer and had since been interned at the Hospital de la Caridad. When I finally went to see her, I could not believe this was the same inflexible woman who had wielded such power and authority during her tyrannical reign over the Buen Pastor prison in Medellín. Lying there in her hospital bed now, completely altered by age and shriveled with the pain and bitterness so easy to read in every wrinkle scoring her face, she was nothing but a sick, old woman.

This decision to see her had required of me an energy I did not think I had. The nun was persistent and called incessantly, so I finally plucked up the courage to face what awaited me. I asked Carmen to go with me. I never went anywhere alone. I knew what the Madre had to say would not be pleasant. That was why I had avoided it. Until now. She wanted to divest herself of that secret that was buried in the darkness of the years, and I was quite content not to conjure it up. By never confronting my husband, I had tried to make a clean break from the past. But if I didn't go see her, Madre Susana would not be able to die; gnawing at her insides was something much more insidious than the cancer they said she had.

She was a shadow of her former self. It was the first time I had ever seen her without her black habit and white coif. She had pulled her coarse hair back in a pathetic little bun that bared her balding, sickly head. Her sunken eyes could no longer summon the stony rigidity that had defined them in years past. I should have been moved to pity. Instead, I was thoroughly repulsed. I stepped backward, my idea was to get out of that room where the air hung heavy with an awful mélange of urine and medicine. But I didn't go. I made a tremendous effort, and leaning on Carmen, I went over to her bed, sat down on a little bench there, and took her hand in mine.

"How do you feel, Madre . . . Susana?"

"Norma, I don't want to waste time, and I neither want nor need your sympathy," she whispered. Her voice was weak, but just as authoritarian as ever. "I called you because I have something important to tell you."

"Is it about Miguel?" I pushed it because I wanted to get it over with as quickly as possible.

"Miguel was the son of a prisoner in Buen Pastor," she clarified, choosing her words carefully.

"I know. And she died, right?"

"No, she didn't die. I don't think she is dead even now."

I stammered that I had trusted my husband, I'd thought he was honest, but the Madre interrupted me abruptly.

"Don't talk nonsense. Listen to me. The woman's name is María Teresa Giraldo. She was in for subversion. She was barely fifteen when she had him. I asked my brother to take the boy while she did her time. That was the initial agreement. Then later he convinced me—he forced me—to get rid of all evidence of the woman's identity. And he adopted the baby as your son."

Suddenly Carmen erupted in sobs. That surprised me more than what the nun was saying.

Madre Susana gulped down some water before she continued: "That woman loved her son. She was no tramp, and she wasn't even guilty of the crime she'd been accused of. She did everything possible to get him back when she got out of prison. But she had no documents to prove her relationship to him, so she never got anywhere. I have in my possession the only paper that I could hide from Ricardo, and it proves Miguel's identity."

I did not want to hear any more. I wanted even less to see a document confirming what I had always suspected. I told her that it wasn't necessary, but she would not be deterred. It was as if her salvation depended on it. She made a tremendous effort and asked a nurse to fetch her a package from a shelf. She shuffled through some papers, found the one she was looking for, and handed it to me, saying: "This is the birth certificate for Miguel Angel Giraldo, issued in prison the day he was born."

As soon as she spoke the words, she was overcome by a coughing fit. The nurse rushed over with a glass of water. I looked over the document she had given me, but it was hard to read the blurred letters on the carbon paper. It was official; it had a seal from the Ministerio de Justicia's Prison Division and recorded the birth of a boy in Medellín's Buen Pastor prison on November 9, 1979. It had been signed by Madre Superiora, the prison secretary, and by one María Teresa Giraldo. I held the document in my hands, and it slowly dawned on me that this paper had nothing to do with me. The people who had signed the yellowed paper meant nothing to me. I had never had any power or control over Miguel's destiny. I didn't even know where he was. I hadn't known for months. The only thing I could bring myself to say was: "And what good does this do me? Why now? I don't need to know this, and you don't gain anything for having told me. Why? Why?" I repeated indignantly.

The nun stared at me callously and responded, her voice almost a whisper: "I don't care what good knowing this does you. Maybe it does you no good at all." She sat up, caught her breath and went on, "But it does me a lot of good to get this weight off my conscience. The only thing I wanted was to save the child from the life he had been born into."

And those words irritated me to no end. My retort was angry: "So that's what you wanted? To deliver him from a horrible path, from a future of crime? Because that's what you deemed was all a prisoner's child had to look forward to? Well, guess what? He didn't escape that fate. After all our meticulous, painstaking care, he is now a criminal. So, Reverend Madre, what you are telling me now does you no good, does me no good, does his alleged mother no good, and does him no good."

I collapsed onto the little bench and buried my head in my hands, trying to purge all the bitterness I had held in for so terribly long. Susana asked the nurse for oxygen. She breathed in deeply through the tank mouthpiece as she settled down into her pillow and closed her eyes. She looked as if a load had just been taken off her shoulders. Carmen took advantage of the pause to hand me a handkerchief. She waited for me to calm down a little, and then loosed what had been caught in her throat:

"I know María Teresa. Mariate."

Carmen was expecting me to blow up, but I had already had enough of secrets, so all I did was mutter: "Ah, you too, Carmen? Another little surprise?"

And then she told us her part of the story. She talked about how her friendship with Mariate had grown through the domestic workers' circuit. Mariate was clearly looking for her son. She told us how they'd kept in touch, and how she hadn't even thought twice about it when she kept Mariate in the know about what Miguel was doing. Toward the end of her story, Carmen clarified that Mariate had never said she was Miguel's mother. But they both just knew what the other person knew, and they had kept the lines of communication open. Now and again Mariate would call from a village called San Juan, where she had been living for the past couple of years.

I almost sprang to my feet with accusations of how she had betrayed me, but when I thought about it for a second, I realized that Carmen was with me because she wanted to be. And if she had intended to betray me, she would have done that a long time ago. Nothing mattered anymore, nothing. What it boiled down to was that this poor woman had lost her son so I could live out my dream of motherhood. Who was to blame? Ricardo, for wreaking this havoc? The nun, for taking the boy from his poor mother to save him from a horrible fate? Life? In the end, we all lost, because Miguel belonged to no one. He didn't even belong to himself.

Carmen helped me pull myself together so I could leave the room with some modicum of dignity. I didn't even say goodbye to Susana. She was exhausted by the tremendous effort she'd made, and had fallen into a light sleep. She couldn't even hear us anymore. I put the paper in my bag and left. I knew I would never go back. It was one long nightmare, calling forth tormented ghosts from my past.

The Tapestry
Mariate

still hadn't decided on the background color for the new tapestry piece. I picked out natural-hue strands from among the range of agave fiber colors scattered across the cabin floor. Earthen jars full of the thick dye we used to tint the raw agave lined the patio. Dyeing agave was laborious, and required effort, preparation, and skill. This particular piece was two meters long and one meter wide. I looked at it as my masterpiece. The undefined sketch of what appeared to be a woman was beginning to take shape in the middle of the tapestry.

Everyone at the San Juan co-op was working hard on at least one piece for the Santafé de Antioquia craft fair. It was the first time we were going, and I knew it was our chance to shine, our chance to show off our new technique with braided, natural-toned agave. Every tapestry showcased our technical skill, mastery, and art, and each motif carried our message of social community and solidarity.

None of us was surprised when our village schoolteacher Marina showed up with two new arrivals, doña Oviedo Patrocinio and doña María Alarcón. She didn't know where to take them, so she brought them to me. They had fled Urabá, and since one of our co-op's missions was to support displaced people, we welcomed them with open arms. We settled in around the earthen jars on the patio to hear their stories.

Doña Oviedo said she'd lived around Córdoba and Antioquia for more than twenty-five years without any problems, but here lately the guerrillas and paramilitaries had been fighting over the territory. When the massacres started, the situation became impossible. She took her family to the village of San Rafael, seeking shelter, a few months ago. There were throngs of displaced people no matter where they turned, and they had nowhere to go. So they squatted in a school and got help from an NGO. But it wasn't long before they were on the move again. The paramilitaries showed up threatening to chop off heads—and her husband's was on the block.

"They had to set an example. My husband was one of the scapegoats," doña Oviedo said. I could tell she was heartbroken, but at the same time she was resigned to her fate.

We waited silently for the next story.

After a while doña María began to talk. She was a *mulata* from Bojayá, in the south of Chocó. Guerrilleros had threatened anyone connected to the paracos. Terrified villagers began to leave the area the day they found bodies floating down the Río Atrato.

"One afternoon men in uniforms went house to house recruiting boys under twenty. They offered to pay them, give them clothes and food. Saying no was not an option. They took my three boys. I don't even know what group they belong to. It's all the same, anyway. They're all a bunch of murderers!"

She blew her nose and dried her tears with the back of her hand, powerless. The rest of us looked at her, wordless.

Then doña Celina spoke, telling them about recent events in our village:

"I don't know what you can do here. We're in the same boat. It hasn't even been two weeks since they killed my husband."

"But then where do we go? We've been running from village to village looking for peace. At every village we go to, we hear the same story," replied doña Oviedo.

"I'm not leaving, no matter what," said doña Celina firmly. "I've made up my mind. The only thing I know is planting my crops and running my shop. I can't picture myself wandering around hungry and begging in some city when everything I have worked for is right here."

"That's what I said, too," agreed doña Oviedo. "But look where I am now . . ."

Just then doña Rosa burst into the room, her face contorted and gasping as she screamed: "Amparo! Amparo! The paras have kidnapped my daughter!"

We were petrified. It was one thing for them to go after men and settle their accounts, but to mess with women, and in this case a young girl, went beyond all wartime codes of conduct. And Amparo was the police chief's daughter, the cutest girl in the village. On top of that, she was my son Gabriel's girlfriend.

"What is the chief saying?" we all demanded at the same time.

"He's like a madman. He has sent word to the military brigade and his superiors, but I don't think they'll do anything. Everyone knows the army won't lift a finger against these asses. They're on the same side."

"And all because my husband wouldn't do what they wanted," doña Rosa sobbed. "I have no idea why he had to be so brave when he has no weapons or anything to fight them with. I saw this coming, but I thought they would go after my husband, not my little girl."

Then doña Marina piped up: "And what are the guerrillas doing?"

I'd had the same thought, too. How long was the guerrilla commando going to swallow the provocations that had gone from humiliating to despicable? What were they waiting for? I thought about Gabriel and what he would do when he heard the news. I knew he was crazy about this girl; he had taken her to my little cabin more than once for their secret rendezvous. At the same time, I feared what was to come. A confrontation between those two irreconcilable sides meant a bloodbath of incalculable proportions, and possibly the end of our little community.

The others saw I was quiet and asked: "Doña Tere, don't you think it's time for the guerrilla to do something?"

"It's not up to me," I said, even though I knew I wasn't convincing.

Doña Rosa came over to me. "I don't know which way to turn. You know what it's like to lose a child. Do something. I'm begging."

I'd come to that village wanting peace and quiet. But we were like doña María and doña Oviedo. It didn't matter where we ran to escape, we could not outrun our destinies.

"No. The guerrillas are not the solution," I spoke clearly. "We have much more power if we act on our own, if we unite all of our power and forces as women."

They all looked at me like I was crazy. And maybe I was. But they had no idea what I had gone through in the guerrilla forces: the constant confrontations and combats, the perpetual fighting, and the bitter taste after every battle. And for what? Never in any one of the combats had there ever been a winner. We were all victim and victimizer at the same time. No one wins in war. We are all losers.

I twisted agave fibers in my fingers as I thought. I knew what the background color would be now. Red. The deepest, reddest red. Burning fire. The fiercest garnet possible. To match my mood.

Victim of Her Own Design

Amparo

"Who sent you? Who did you come here for?"

"No one. I swear. I came on my own," I told them again and again.

⊚

As soon as she rounded the bend into paramilitary territory, Amparo knew that her plan was an epic failure. What on earth was she thinking? That Chacho would fall at her feet and suddenly be at her beck and call? She had no idea how to explain why she was there, and they all thought she was part of some guerrilla plan to throw them off. They had her tied to a chair blindfolded. The rope was cutting into her wrists and the blindfold was crushing her temples. But the worst was all the shouting and obscenities.

"Blow her away!" one yelled. "Better yet, do her, buddy, *hermano*. Just look at her! Damn, she's hot." Some were laughing, and others were making sick jokes, pawing at her breasts or between her legs.

"Shit, she's a guerrilla whore! She's with some guy they call Mono."

At last she heard Chacho's voice. He stopped them short and ordered all of them to leave him alone with her. They did as they were told, joking as they left: "He wants her all to himself. Leave some for us, old man!"

I felt him come closer. He looked me over and then in a rare act of mercy took off my blindfold. He spoke, but the tone of his voice was different.

"Do you have any idea the position you've put us in by coming to our camp?" he said.

I couldn't see well right after he took off the blindfold, but as my eyes came into focus and I looked into his eyes, I knew that even in such an awful situation, they melted my heart.

"I get it," I murmured.

"So, tell me the truth. What are you here for? Who sent you, and what do you want?"

"Okay. But untie me, please. I can't talk like this."

Chacho loosened the rope that was tormenting my wrists, but he didn't take it completely off. When I felt him relax a little, I knew he was ready to listen and so gave him a summary of what had brought me there.

"I thought that since you were, well, how can I put this . . . nice to me and . . . you remember the fiesta? I thought that, well . . . I thought that I could talk to you."

"Talk to me? Why?"

"To ask you to leave us alone, to stop killing people, to leave the village."

Chacho looked at me in surprise. There was finally a glint of humanity flickering in his eyes. But it was fleeting. His authoritarian tone returned and he said: "You think I want to be here? I am responsible for getting rid of the guerrillas; they have taken over the entire territory! This village has been sold; even your father, the police chief himself, has been sold. You all do what those assholes tell you to do."

"That's not true," I dared contradict him.

"Even you—you are that guerrillero's girl."

"Mono? He's not . . ."

"Don't tell me you don't know. You may be naive, but you're not stupid."

It was surprising. Despite his gruff demeanor he had good manners, unlike the killers who surrounded him. He seemed like a decent guy, maybe he even came from a good family. He wasn't crude, and he didn't lay a finger on me. Chacho looked at me intensely and handed down my sentence:

"You realize I can't let you go, right? You've walked right into your own trap. Work with me, and nothing bad will happen to you. And don't try to manipulate me with your silly seductions; I am not a man schoolgirls can trifle with. Your being here is a good card for us to play in our negotiations, and you asked for this."

His words were harsh and I was petrified. Yet his mysterious eyes were still relentlessly alluring.

Sons of War

Mariate

Gabriel came crashing through the cabin door in a panic. He'd found out Amparo was being held and now, finally, the guerrillas were preparing an attack. He was afraid for her—one false move and she could be dead. But something else was bugging him, too.

"What was she thinking? We interrogated her friend Cristina. She told us Amparo didn't go to hang out with her friends this afternoon. She said Amparo had been acting weird; she barely said a word, like she was up to something. Like she had a date with that . . . asshole."

"But why do you think she would go meet him?"

"I don't know, Mamá. I don't know. They were dancing at the fiesta. I still can't get that picture out of my head."

"You're jealous, hijo. No one would dream of going to see that guy after everything that's happened in this town."

But I wasn't all that convinced, myself. I only said what I did as a salve for Gabriel's injured pride and anger. I knew he was capable of anything, and his age was definitely clouding his thinking.

"You know Rafa is coming to town, right?" he blurted out unexpectedly.

"Rafael? Your brother? Why?"

"He's coming with his gang, helping with weapons and troops."

"What troops?" I asked, alarmed.

"Mamá, please! You already know this!" was his curt reply.

Well, yes; I knew. Even if I didn't really want to. My third son, Rafa, my little boy, the one the commando had ordered me to leave with my sister when he was just a tiny baby, was an ache deep down inside me. He was one of the kids who'd joined the Medellín gangs and become a hit man, demanding top dollar. It was the horrific legacy Pablo Escobar had left us.

Gabriel said goodbye with a simple "See you," as he slammed the door behind him. I got nothing more out of him. I could have asked more about his brother, but for what? He wouldn't want to see me, and I didn't want to see him, either. I could not stand what he had become.

Not that I could say I was thrilled about the idea of Gabriel as a guerrilla fighter, either. But that was his life, the only one he had ever known. He'd always been in this senseless war, even if it went on now for very different reasons than when it began. Sure, I saw him a lot when he camped with the front that controlled the region, but there were times I couldn't recognize him. He was barely eighteen, but he looked like an old man who'd been run through the wringer. His face was scarred by violence, and his green eyes had seen so much they were forever stained. Nothing could shock them anymore.

◎

Mariate jumped when a Telecom messenger appeared at her door with an important message from a woman named Carmen. She dropped everything to go to a public phone center to call Medellín.

That was when Carmen told her about Madre Susana's deathbed regrets and her call to Señora Norma to finally reveal the secret that would not let her die. Norma's reaction was heartbreaking. She had always thought her adopted son's biological mother was dead. She had been lied to as well. Now that she knew about Mariate and had thought it over, Norma wanted to meet her.

◎

"For what?"

"I don't know. It's her conscience," Carmen explained. "The woman suffered a lot. The guerrillas killed her father and her husband. She lives alone, abandoned. Miguel left a long time ago, and she has no idea where he is. Maybe it's a way for her to get answers."

Her words pierced me to the depths of my soul. Now I was supposed to feel compassion? No one had ever shown me any.

"What good does it do her for us to meet?"

"Maybe she just wants back the son she lost, like you do."

"So, Carmen, you're saying you knew the whole time that Miguel was my son? How?"

116

"I always knew, amiga. I knew the very day Miguel came to doña Norma's, all wrapped up in a handmade ruanita, that it could only have been made by strong, loving hands. And when I met you and I saw your work, well, then my hunch was confirmed. I understood you; we became friends and I kept you up to date on Miguel, but . . ."

"But what?"

"But I couldn't turn on my boss. Please understand, amiga."

I took a deep breath and enunciated each word that followed very slowly: "Tell your señora she can rest easy. I have no bitterness in my heart against her or anyone. I had three boys, and I lost them all to this war. This damned war. Your señora and the whole Restrepo clan, the Madre Superiora included, can live or die as they choose, in peace."

"Madre Susana died two days ago."

I felt a knot in my throat. I could only stammer: "May God forgive her!"

"Before she died she gave the señora Miguel's birth certificate."

And those words effectively unraveled the knot that had been stuck in my throat.

"His what, his birth certificate?" I could not take any more. It was too much. I burst into a torrent of indignant sobs. How many times had she told me no! She even swore the damned certificate had never existed, making sure that every single office I went to as I tried to prove I was his mother would tell me no. Carmen listened without a word. It was a while before she ventured to say: "Mariate, it's not too late. Let doña Norma come visit you. She has been through a lot, too. It will do you both good. Maybe it's not too late to get Miguel back."

For a second I pictured meeting the son I had lost twenty-two years ago again. But I felt the same about him as I did about Rafa. It was better not to see him. God knows what he had become.

Just then doña Marina ran in, interrupting the call as she screamed, her chest heaving: "Mariate! Mariate! The paras have taken over the police station and the mayor's office! They're going house to house, turning everyone out. They have a list of people they're looking for. Get out of here! You're on the list! They're all riled up because the guerrillas ambushed them this morning. There was a firefight!"

"Where are the guerrillas now?"

"They just put up checkpoints on the edge of town, and they've blocked all the roads. There's no way out."

I heard the explosions coming from the village. I asked doña Marina to go with me to get water and wood for supplies. On the way to the river, we ran into other women, crying hysterically because their husbands had been rooted out of their homes early that morning. They had left their parcels of land, fleeing with their kids and a few belongings. They had nowhere to go.

"Everyone, come up to my house," I told them. "Bring whatever supplies you can find. We are going to hole up in my den."

All that military training I had had during my years in the guerrillas was coming in handy. I knew all about holing up, ambushes, and defense strategies. I knew about weapons, too, and I would go so far as to use the revolver I had hidden in the bottom of a trunk, if I had to.

"The first thing we have to do is set up a stockade," I ordered the women. "Then we drench cloths in oil, gas or whatever combustible we can find. And matches. We need matches and candles."

Soon women with their little ones in tow began arriving at my cabin. I set about organizing them and assigned them jobs. They all followed my lead.

"Hurry," I ordered, "there's no time to waste. We need to make it look like no one is here. We can't call attention to ourselves, and we have to stay calm."

Big drops of rain began to fall as the village women ran here and there, preparing. Before long the downpour forced them to hunker down in the tiny cabin. The explosions from the village were muted in the din of the storm. Some women started reciting prayers, while kids, caught between curious and scared, hid under the skirts of their mothers and grandmothers. Something was happening; something very serious was about to go down.

Suddenly my conversation with Carmen came back to mind. I could truthfully say that long ago I had lost any trace of bitterness or resentment. What mattered most now was making sure that every one of those helpless people clinging to me, as if I were a lifeboat, would be okay.

The Checkpoint
Norma

"What do you think we should do with these old ladies?" the soldier asked. "I don't see the issue. Make them go back, like everyone else."

"But, Commander, they say they know Mono's mother, Mariate. They say it's an emergency, and since doña Mariate lives near the mountain, we should let them through."

The guerrilla boss stood at the checkpoint, looking at us. I had driven for three hours through the mountains in areas that were not protected by the army, something I never would have tried under normal circumstances. That morning an old compañero of Miguel's from the military brigade had given me some life-changing information that convinced me to go to San Juan to find Miguel's mother. I was so obsessed with seeing her that my fear and suspicion had dissipated. Carmen had decided to come on the adventure with me. She wanted to find her friend as much as I did. Maybe more. The commander came over to us; he had a look on his face that was confused and irritated at the same time. I rolled down my window, and he began to question me.

"What's the issue, doña? Can't you see this is a war zone? Get outta here right away, and we won't hurt you."

I took off my dark glasses and said, respectfully but firmly.

"Señor . . . ?"

"Commander. Call me Commander."

"I have not come all this way just to turn back. I fully understand the danger we are in, but I am asking you to let us through to see Señora María Teresa Giraldo, anyway. We have a very urgent matter to discuss with her. We don't need to go into town, and the thought of meddling in your war hasn't even crossed my mind. Let us go through."

The man wouldn't budge, so she added: "Look, if you're going to kidnap me, I'm sorry, but it would be a waste of time because there is not one person who will give even a peso for me. The guerrillas have already taken everything I ever had. If you're going to kill me, it'll save me the trouble of having to do it myself. The only thing I ask is that you let me talk to doña María Teresa before you do either of those things."

The commander turned his menacing face to her. He was puzzled. He obviously didn't know what to do; the mere presence of this woman intimidated him. For a moment, she thought he was going to let them through, but that would have been asking too much of a fool with power. He looked the car over. It was plain to see he was itching to have it.

"Only something really important could make a señora speak to me with such disrespect," he said sarcastically. But there was also deceit in his voice. "Do you think you're dealing with some peon on your hacienda or what?" He looked at her with intense hatred. There were years and years of subjugation and rancor behind the commander façade on his sallow face.

"Oh, no, Señora. If you don't want to turn back, then we'll keep you here. You and your car. And your friend, too. Oh, wait, she can't be your friend," he corrected himself when he saw Carmen. "She's your maid, more like."

At that point Norma finally understood the magnitude of her recklessness, and she tried to protest. But it was too late. The commander ordered the barely pubescent boys in uniform to tie them up. They led them into a shack at the side of the road. It was a multipurpose hut, at once checkpoint command, combat headquarters, barracks, and shelter. It was stocked with military supplies, and equipment was piled up in a corner.

"Watch her, boys," he warned. "This is a golden cow. She could come in pretty handy."

Their hands and feet were tied up with line made of cabuya. They were left sprawled over some backpacks and putrid mattresses in the equipment corner.

"Listen," said Carmen, breaking her silence. "Could you at least tell Mariate or Mono we're here? Don't be a jerk, compañero! This could end up helping you, too."

The commander ignored Carmen; he was busy preparing for something. Groups of men in uniform were lining up around him while he gave orders left and right. They were all very careful around their boss, putting rifles and clips together and taking them apart again, loading munitions, and gathering together all they needed for war. There was a strong scent of battle in the air, and it stoked the men that much more.

Then a motorcycle convoy roared into the checkpoint carrying young men clad in leather jackets and dark glasses, studded boots, and helmets inlaid with mother-of-pearl. They were all soaked to the skin.

"We made it," one said arrogantly as he took off his helmet.

Several guerrilleros jumped up and grabbed their weapons, aiming at the new arrivals. Norma could hear the guerrilla commander's nasal voice: "Who are you, and what do you want?"

"My name is Rafa. These are my men. Mono sent for us. Reinforcements from Medellín's Commune Thirteen."

The commander got on his walkie-talkie and radioed someone before he answered.

"I am Commander César. If your story is true, I am your commander. You have to obey my orders and mine alone."

Norma peeked through a crack in the window and gasped at all the weapons those boys had. She watched the commander and saw the unbridled greed written on his face as his furrowed brow smoothed out into sharp desire. They were young, yes, but those boys probably had more war experience than the most seasoned guerrilleros. She was surprised and horrified by the age of the boys in both groups. They barely had any peach fuzz on their faces, and the sharp pitch of boyhood still clung to their voices. Their loss of innocence was only visible in their eyes. Those dark glasses hid the hostility and malice of those who know no compassion.

Commander César barked out orders to give the new arrivals uniforms. He took their weapons and traded them for some of lesser quality. Then he confiscated their cell phones, electronics, and counterfeit Ray-Bans, and made them spit out the gum they were chomping on so confidently. Then he had them put on rubber boots that went all the way up their calves.

"These boots are horrendous!" Rafa protested insolently.

"Complaining, whining, and crying are prohibited. This is war, not a pussy game!" César snarled harshly to bring home the weight of his authority.

Night descended. Despite the downpour, several combat troops were headed into town. It was looking like there was going to be a gruesome confrontation. And there was Norma. Witness, victim, and/or mediator.

At Their Posts

Mariate

It got darker and darker, and it rained harder and harder. The guerrilla commandos were spread out all over and controlled most of the village. The auto-defensas held the town square and strategic points like the Banco Agrario, the police station, the church, and the health clinic.

The villagers were caught in the middle. Those who had managed to escape before morning had left all their belongings and were now hiding somewhere up in the mountains. Others had sought shelter at Mariate's; most were hunkered down in their houses, waiting for the paramilitaries and the guerrilleros to fight it out and massacre anyone who was unlucky enough to be caught in the crossfire. That was when what always happened would happen: One side would declare victory, and the surviving villagers would have to go along with whatever that side said. Either way, there was no hope. That's what had happened in other villages, like San Pedro, Valdivia, Yarumal, Santa Rosa, Taraza; the list went on and on. Pueblos wiped out and dislocated, endless caravans of displaced people flowing into the urban centers. Campesinos and villagers alike left everything without knowing why or understanding how they had gotten caught up in a war that was not winnable. It dragged on for decades, always spawning more and more hatred. Injury and retaliations were handed down from generation to generation in an endless chain of misery and blood.

No Choice

Norma

Norma and Carmen still didn't know what was going to happen to them. The men were so busy they seemed to have forgotten about them. They hadn't forgotten the women's car, though. Norma and Carmen could hear it chugging back and forth, transporting equipment and soldiers.

Later that night a platoon arrived, led by some guy they called Mono. Carmen told Norma he was María Teresa's other son. Norma tried to study his face for some resemblance to Miguel, but it was impossible for her to distinguish his features in the shadows. He was just another rabid young man, probably recruited by force or with empty promises. That was how guerrilleros spent their lives.

The ladies gleaned information from the conversations around them. That was how they found out the paras had taken over the police station and were holding the police chief, the Banco Agrario manager, the health center staff, security guards, and public servants hostage there. Commander César reminded his troops that they had to proceed with caution. No one wanted a bloody slaughter to claim the lives of village officials; many of them were allies of the guerrillas. Their mission was to rescue the hostages before the paramilitaries unleashed the massacre foretold.

César said it was no secret that the guerrillas had the upper hand: They had more troops and better weapons. The villagers had supplied the guerrillas with ample food. But it was different for the people being held at the police station. Their food and water would not last very long. The paramilitary commando didn't have enough to feed them all and maintain hygiene for so many in such cramped quarters. The fear was they would start killing hostages. The guerrillas could not allow that to happen. They would have to attack by surprise in the wee hours of the morning.

Just then, Mono saw us. We could tell he was asking about us, because he was pointing at us. Someone told him we were hostages; the commander interrupted: "Yeah, they came with some story that they're friends of your mamá. You know them?"

The young man came closer to get a better look and shook his head no.

Carmen burst out in a torrent of words, "I'm Carmen, your mamá is a friend of mine. You're Gabriel; I met you when you were little. Please, tell her we're here from Medellín. We have something very important to tell her. An urgent message."

"What's the message?"

"We have to tell her in person," I said, interrupting. "Could you at least let us talk to doña María Teresa by phone?"

"What do we do, hermano?" César asked Mono.

"You know my mamá doesn't have a phone. I don't know these old ladies. She never hung out with this kind of people. This is probably a trap."

"Hombre, don't be that way!" Carmen insisted. "Do you really think we'd dare set foot in this hell if we didn't have a really good reason?"

"What's the reason?" asked the commander. "If you tell us why your boss has ventured into these parts, I'll even let her go see doña Tere."

My lips were sealed and so was our fate. They had no time for more protests or negotiations, and César and his men scattered to other parts of the camp. We spent that night huddled in a damp corner of the nasty little hut, the tension in the air trickling in through the roof, along with the pounding rain.

Just before dawn, I could feel someone walking outside the hut. I pulled myself up to sitting and looked through the crack in the window. That's how I overheard some of their conversation.

"It's me, Rafa, hermano. Lower your weapon."

"When did you get here?" It was Mono's voice.

"We've been under Commander César since this afternoon. What a guy! You didn't tell me guerrilleros were such assholes."

"What were you expecting? This is war, hermano!"

"Oh, okay. So, what are you fighting for this time?"

They were silent for a while. Then they lit a cigarette, and I could see their shadows in the flickering light.

"Hey, why don't you tell me how a city boy like you decided to come out here to the boonies?"

"Man, they have it out for us . . . They want to kill us, dude, that's the thing. Me and my men, we need to disappear for a while. You think the old man would let us join the front for a while?"

"Only if you're not a jerk, and you're tough as steel, and you don't go getting yourself into trouble. You can't be complaining or screwing with the command. Keep your eyes open! You got it? And now, go get some rest. Tomorrow's battle is going to be brutal. Hey, and when this shit's all over, go by Mamá's; she wants to see you."

"Mamá? We haven't seen each other in years and years . . ."

I couldn't make out the rest of the conversation because they moved out of earshot. Carmen and I looked at each other. So Rafa was Miguel's other brother?

I got no sleep that night; I was worn out, exhausted by the harsh conditions. What in the world was I, Norma de Restrepo, doing surrounded by killers and murderers in the middle of a war that was not mine? Who told me to stick my nose into this mess?

Mediator

Amparo

It was just as Chacho had predicted: Amparo was now their bargaining chip. She was both bait and mediator for all that was to come.

The chief had no choice but to surrender with his entire force when the auto-defensas showed up at the station, waving Amparo out in front like a flag. The entire police corps now followed their orders. No one put up a fight when the paras went from house to house, detaining every village official. Except the mayor. They didn't detain the mayor. The police station became their fortress. And there they were, submissive, waiting for who knows what.

But Chacho was growing desperate. When he planned the operation, he forgot to think about how long they would be there. Now the hunger and other needs the hostages had, combined with the stench, began to be a bigger problem than the confrontation itself. As night fell, he had to set most of the hostages free. Then he ordered his men to bring food from nearby houses, but he could tell it was still not going to be enough for so many people. They would run out within a day. The officers were trained to make do with short rations during wartime, but the village officials weren't. They were used to their big meals of meat, beans, and arepa, three times a day. Chacho ordered them to make a huge kettle of coffee with panela. He had them pass out some arepa with cheese. That tided the hostages over for a while. The chief could see the comandante's problem, and took advantage of it to rankle him.

"My esteemed Comandante, how long do you plan to keep us like this? You're stuck in your own trap, can't you see?"

Chacho was weighed down by exhaustion from the stress of the day, and this time he held his tongue. But the comments had clearly hit their mark.

The police chief had experience with things like this, and knew what he was talking about.

"Why don't you just kill us and get it all over with? I mean, look, your troops are tired and you don't have the operational capacity to keep this up for very long. It's a waste of military resources."

Comandante wouldn't budge. He stared out the window as the chief's critiques got sharper and more biting.

"I don't get why you aren't just slaughtering us like you do in every other village. Everyone knows you go in shooting. What's the difference here? Why don't you do that? What are you waiting for? For the guerrillas to come rescue us? No, hombre, you're on the wrong track. That won't work with the guerrillas."

"Shut the hell up!" Comandante shouted, enraged. He got up, took out his revolver, and led by primal instinct, aimed it right at the chief's temple. His hand was shaking.

"Shut it right now if you don't want me to blast your head off!"

The chief went mute. That feeling he had that the man at the other end of the revolver would not be able to pull the trigger had completely evaporated. Comandante lowered his weapon and stalked out of the room.

Trying to calm himself down, he decided to take some time to inspect the other hostages. He was still shaking when he came back in and walked over to one side of the office. I was kneeling in a corner. Chacho took a deep breath to compose himself, and looked at me.

He moved with a start and motioned for me to follow him to a room upstairs, where his officials were waiting. He ordered them out. We were alone. I was afraid he was going to shoot me, but he was calm as he started talking.

"This is very serious business, Amparo, and I need your help. You and I understand each other, but I need to know for sure that you are on my side. That you won't stab me in the back. Can I count on you?"

I nodded slowly, but I couldn't see how he would need my help.

"Tomorrow is going to be really hard. There is going to be a vicious fight. I'm pretty sure it will be a bloodbath on both sides. You might not believe me, but this is not what I wanted to go down. If I had my choice, I would have avoided it. It all depends on you. Do what I tell you, and we will avoid a massacre."

I nodded, but I still didn't fully comprehend. Then, suddenly, all my fear of his power melted into compassion. He had sat down next to me and dropped

130

his head into his hands. I mustered the courage to ask: "Chacho, can you explain to me what you're doing in this war? You seem like such an awesome guy. What in the world happened that made you end up here?"

And I don't know how, but that arrogant man everyone was so afraid of just opened his soul and let loose what was weighing so heavily on him.

The deep wound carved into his heart when he saw his father murdered festered still. He could not forgive himself for not having had the courage to stand up to the killers, even though he knew that he would have paid for it with his own life. And every day he thought that if he only had it to do over again, he would hurl his body in front of his father's to save him.

"It doesn't make any sense to live with this kind of pain," he said.

He relived the horror of the threats foretelling the murders. They were spending the summer on his grandparents' finca when the first ones came. A FARC front had taken over the zone and came by demanding their customary "vaccine," a tax that ranch owners paid in cash or in livestock so the guerrillas would leave them in peace. Every vaccine came with a new condition. The ranchers were desperate.

General Restrepo had asked the brigade for protection, but got nothing because the brigade said it didn't know where the guerrilla force was operating. The Alvarez family had been losing land and livestock for a while, keeping the guerrillas happy, and they refused to pay one peso more. They pulled together with other ranchers in the Magdalena Medio to form auto-defensa groups. His father was one of the leaders.

And after that there were threats from both sides. First, they tried to kidnap his grandfather. The guards routed out the kidnappers in time and whisked him away to safety. Then the threats came in messages and phone calls. His mother begged them not to go back to the finca, but both his father and his grandfather were adamantly opposed to giving the land to the guerrillas. They were sure their allies would come through for them. But they were wrong.

One night, they were eating dinner on the terrace at the hacienda when a group of men, armed to the gills, showed up out of the blue, chanting their slogans. By the time they realized what was going on, the bodyguards had already been taken out and the entire family was defenseless. Chacho recounted exactly where everyone was at the table: His grandfather was at the head, his mother at her father's right hand, his father across from his mother, and he himself to the right of his mother. He was sixteen. Ten guerrilleros parked right in front of them, brandishing their weapons. The rest had scattered throughout the finca. There was no way out. Obviously, a mole had wormed his way in with the ranch hands to help the guerrillas take over the hacienda. They could only have done this if they knew intimate details of the land, the house, and their activities. The leader aimed straight at both the grown men. Then he addressed Chacho's father defiantly.

"General, we know what you've been up to. We know you have connections with MAS, the narcos, and the paras. Now, you know neither you nor all your influence can stop us. One day in the not-too-distant future we are going to lead this country, but for now, rats like you can go to hell."

He signaled, and his men emptied their machine guns into Chacho's grandpa, *abuelo* Alvarez, and Chacho's father, General Restrepo.

"I will never forget the panic I felt in that moment, I swear," Chacho said. "It's replayed over and over in my mind, looping back around to play again. I'm obsessed. Ever since that moment, I have been empty. The only thing I can remember of what happened before I passed out is my mamá screaming hysterically."

After the murders, he tried to navigate the tunnels of sorrow and grief. He clung to the military brigade for a good bit, hoping it would give him answers and support him in avenging his father's death. The question that nagged at him, though, was: what good did so much military training do him if he could not even defend the one he loved the most?

"Why didn't I jump on those guys before they started shooting? Why him and not me? Why did they let me live?" he looked at me in desperation, as if I had the answer.

"So, what did the brigade do? I mean, your father dedicated his life to the military."

Chacho was visibly embittered. He said the army did absolutely nothing about the brutal murders. All the army did was host a ceremony in his father's memory, a funeral march from the mayor's office to the Medellín cathedral. Grandiloquent speeches, military honors, and booming cannons celebrated the illustrious deceased. But it wasn't enough to quench his thirst for vengeance.

"They had this extravagant funeral with full military honors, and then swept everything under the rug, spun it into a spiral of silence and immunity. Just like every other headline in the nation," he said.

"Didn't they open an investigation?" I asked.

"Nothing. They made stern condemnations in statements for all the big newspapers, and they wrote obituaries in his honor. It is an outrage, but to officials in this country, impunity is as important as the tricolored flag they drape over the coffins of our dead."

It wasn't until after he got promoted to lieutenant that he realized the army would never help him. International human rights organizations were watching the military like a hawk because of its past abuses. Officials were under tight scrutiny; they were severely punished if there was just a suspicion they'd stepped out of line. That had made the fight against the guerrillas harder. Counter-guerrilla commandos were sometimes able to take over a camp or win a battle against one of the guerrilla groups, but then the district attorney's office had to come in to identify the victims. That could take days or even weeks, and the soldiers had to remain in the area the entire time. And then they ran the risk of being ambushed by other groups. Situations like that had triggered deep unrest among the soldiers; they were frustrated. They could not complete their missions.

He'd shut himself off and debated about what to do for months; he'd had negative after negative from his battalion. Finally, he decided to join the auto-defensas. His father might not have known it, but he had forged the path for him. He already had the connections, and besides, they had already contacted him to tell him what everyone already knew: His father had been killed for supporting the paras operating in the Magdalena Medio.

He made his decision in secret. He told no one. He even left his mamá completely in the dark. Of course, he did not tell his military commanders. He joined block thirteen under Comandante Fidel.

As he approached the end of his story, the man before me had changed. He was no longer the para commander who'd taken over the village. He was just a man. Flesh and blood. A young man consumed by a desperation that sapped his spirit because he was powerless in the face of death after death. He could do nothing against an endless cycle of vengeance avenging vengeance. I don't know how it happened. The only thing I could do was hold out my arms to him. He seemed resigned, but he yielded to me as I rocked him gently. That is how the wee morning hours crept up on us.

The Refuge

Mariate

There were several guerrilla fronts stationed at strategic points throughout the village, and the paras controlled the police station. That night it was grim and dismal at every single post, without exception.

The ladies at doña Tere's had slept little, if at all, and had been frenetically busy all night. The younger women were painting enormous signs, while the older ones set about making arepas and hot chocolate over the wood fire, and the kids hauled pots of water up from the creek for basic needs.

Like ants, they worked away. The schoolteacher had taken on making the biggest posters; she had beautiful handwriting! Others were on walkie-talkies getting information on what was happening in town from those who hadn't fled. The older women and kids were either cleaning or pasting sticks to the backs of posters. The clock on the church steeple had not yet struck seven that morning, and they were ready. A group of people arrived from the guerrilla checkpoint while they were having breakfast. They were led by Padre Leandro. First the guerrillas had detained him, but then they sent him on to the refuge. He'd come early that morning, as he did every Sunday, to hold Mass. This time he brought news:

"The guerrillas are stationed at every corner of the square. They're going to attack any time now."

"But they can't attack just like that. They know our men are inside there, too!" one lady said.

"They don't care about that. When it comes down to it, the guerrillas forget who their friends are and mow down anyone in their path," doña Celina said firmly.

"Oh, I almost forgot!" the priest interrupted. "There are a couple of women at the checkpoint who say they're friends of yours. They were detained on their way to your place yesterday afternoon."

"Really? Who are they?" I asked, surprised.

"I saw them briefly when they were patting me down at the checkpoint. They're from Medellín. They begged me to tell you that they had an urgent message for you."

Who from Medellín could want to see me? My sister, maybe? I wondered, but the news was quickly buried under chaotic preparations and the thousands of things I had going on.

"We have to hurry!" Marina yelled. "I hear explosions coming from the village now. The fighting's started!"

Some of the villagers started saying hushed prayers, while the rest rushed around doing whatever had to be done. They fastened sticks to the finished posters with ribbons and cords. The posters looked like flags.

"There's no time to lose!" I shouted. "Everyone to your post!"

Before we started down to the village, I snuck into my room, and from the bottom of my trunk I pulled the gun that I kept for emergencies. A .45 Magnum.

Padre Leandro led the younger women out in front as our vanguard. The older ladies and kids followed. Everyone carried a poster or a flag. The padre took his place out in front, leading the caravan and chanting a prayer.

The Battle

Amparo

Day broke. The sky had cleared, and now the hostages in the police station could see they were surrounded. Guerrilleros were standing ready at their combat posts all around the square. You could hear the rat-a-tat-tat of different weapons, the snap of safeties being released, and the clicking of magazines being loaded reverberating through the plaza. Tension was so thick you could cut it with a knife. And the villagers waited, stewing in their prayers, sweat, and tears. Then the first shots began to hit the building. Back at the station, they were waiting for Comandante's orders.

But Chacho did nothing, so the chief got in his face.

"Are you going to let them slaughter us all, just like that? Do something!"

Silence.

"Señor Comandante," he ordered, "untie us and we can help you. My officers and I will shoot from one side of the building, while your men shoot from the other. We need to have a defense strategy. Give us back our weapons."

Comandante obeyed. He freed the hostages; the officers ran, one or two to a window, and began to fire.

The crackle of flying bullets sounded through the San Juan Plaza as both sides fought furiously. The guerrillas were perched behind the ceiba trees and the statue of Bolívar on the square. Little by little they were gaining ground and moving in on all sides of the building.

I looked out through a crack in the window to watch the firefight. On the one hand, I was terrified, but on the other, I was excited to witness this event. My mother told me to get away from the window and pray with her. When I didn't pay her any mind, an elderly woman told me: "Señorita Amparo, there is nothing to see here! I've been watching this same war play out the same way for decades. The only difference is the year. It's like a bad movie they remake every twenty years, swapping out old actors with new ones who are even nastier."

A Drink in the Nick of Time

Norma

The rat-a-tat-tat of the guns sounded oppressive from the makeshift barracks where Carmen and I were held. Desperation was overcoming me. What use was all my bravery in venturing out, if I couldn't do what I had set out to do? I absolutely had to get to that village. María Teresa didn't matter anymore, nothing did. I had to get free and run. Carmen noticed the guerrilleros had disappeared. We figured they were all in combat now. But we were still gagged and tied, and couldn't figure out how to get free.

We saw a glimmer of hope flash before us when the priest showed up early that morning. Maybe he would give María Teresa the message after all, and someone would come looking for us.

I went over and over our options in my head, as I tried to work loose the twine wrapped so tightly that it dug into my hands and legs. Carmen scooted over and leaned against my back, and we tried to untie each other the way they do in the movies. It was a desperate attempt, and it was futile.

While we were busy doing that, a Postobón pop truck drove up. No one was manning the checkpoint now, but the driver still couldn't get through because there were tree trunks lying across the road. He got out to move them; we saw our chance and screamed through the gags as loud as we could. The man stopped and looked around; then he came closer and poked his face through the window to see where the noise was coming from. He saw us and came even closer—we could see he was afraid, but he was also determined to help.

It took him all of ten seconds to free us. The only thing he asked us was: "What's going on here?"

"The guerrillas have taken over the village. They're in full-out war. Get out of here before you get caught up in this, too," I warned.

"Ah, but before you go, could you leave us a pop? May the Lord repay you," begged Carmen.

Ah, Carmen. She never forgot about details—like survival. Me, on the other hand, I couldn't remember the last thing I ate or drank. And I was so nervous that when I got up and tried to run, I fell over on my first step. I was stiff from being tied up for so long.

The Postobón truck driver immediately offered to get us out of there. Part of me wanted to accept his offer, but the stronger part of me begged him to leave us at the edge of the village instead. The man could not understand why I would refuse and kept insisting:

"Are you sure, doña? You don't want to get out of this shithole? Look how bad things are; just listen to the guns."

"I am sure, yes. And I so appreciate your offer, but I know what I'm doing. I am completely sure."

He looked at me curiously and then dropped us off at the edge of the village. As he said goodbye, I could tell from his face he was convinced that I was possessed, crazy, or mad. Or all three.

Carmen and I ran to the village square. We followed the pack-and-thud of the bullets that got louder and louder the closer we came.

Face to Face
Amparo

It wasn't long before the police station was surrounded by guerrilleros, shooting at it from all sides. The police and auto-defensas inside the station returned their fire. But they knew they were trapped and running out of ammo.

The guerrillas' advantage was so great, they were now rattling at the doors, about to storm the building. That was when the chief went to Chacho.

"Hombre, we've lost. Surrender. We're surrounded. We're all going to die."

"No, never!" shouted Comandante.

Then he looked at me. I remembered his words from the night before. I stood up obediently, and walked over to him. I looked at him, my eyes pleading.

"Trust me," he said.

That was the first time he'd ever been so kind with me.

He took me by the arm and led me down the stairs to the main door. My mother saw what was going on and begged: "No! Don't take Amparo, no! For the love of God!"

My father tried to stop us.

"Take me!"

And I was the one who answered them.

"Papá, calm down. Nothing bad is going to happen to me."

Chacho opened the door and pushed me out slowly, dodging bullets as we went. He was directly behind me; I was his shield.

And suddenly I was facing thousands of men who didn't know whether to lower their weapons or save Chacho the trouble and just kill me. I couldn't see, the sun was so bright. All I could see was an amorphous mass of fighters in the middle of the square.

Chacho barked: "Stop the attack or I'll kill her!"

He pressed the ice-cold barrel of the gun up to my forehead. He wouldn't do it. I heard his words echoing in my head: "Trust me, trust me . . ." I said them to myself over and over, to quell the terror that was bubbling up inside me.

Then my vision cleared, and I could see Mono. He was beyond furious, pushing through to the front lines. Someone tried to hold him back, but he was single-minded.

"Let her go, asshole!" he growled.

Some guy who was probably the guerrilla commander meted out my sentence: "Kill her if you want! She's not one of us!"

"March!" he ordered. "The station is ours!"

Chacho's plan had flopped. Guerrilleros rushed into the building, and I was smack in the middle of the attack. What was Chacho going to do? He had to kill me to make good on his threat! If he didn't, he would lose the last shred of dignity left in him. I could feel his pulse through the gun pressing into my forehead.

While he was making up his mind, we heard voices coming down the hill along the church side of the street. A caravan of women carrying posters painted with the slogan "NO WAR" marched boldly right into the thick of the battle, chanting at the top of their lungs:

"No more war! No more hate! No more blood!"

The bullets stopped. None of the fighters knew what to do. They looked around, bewildered, as the women marched right into the middle of the square, all fired up. They used their posters as shields and stopped the advance of the guerrillas. In all that chaos of men and women on the square, I caught sight of Mono. He'd managed to break through the masses and pounced on Chacho, enraged.

His pounce threw us both to the ground. Somehow, I managed to crawl free of the melee while they went at it one on one. Seconds later, Chacho had already overcome Mono. He was straddling him, and the gun that seconds ago was aimed at my forehead was now aimed right into Mono's neck.

I closed my eyes because I just could not watch what was coming, and I let loose a howl that was quickly drowned out in the clamor of the women on the square.

No More War! No More Hate!
No More Blood!
Mariate

The priest led our convoy while we chanted as if we were reciting a responsive prayer. We waved our posters—our shields—and shouted: "No more war! No more hate! No more blood!" And we pushed stubbornly ahead, straight into the battle.

And the shooting seemed to let up.

Commander César was the first to start barking orders.

"What's going on? Get outta here! Don't stop, men! Don't even slow down! Keep fighting! Everyone at your post!" he shouted desperately.

This was the very moment they should be taking the police station over and crushing the auto-defensas.

"We've got this. Move!" he insisted.

No one was listening, though. They were all mesmerized by the vision of the women taking over the battlefield so brazenly, chanting with conviction: "No more war! No more war! We want our men, our sons, our husbands, our fathers. No more war!"

César knew it was pointless to try to force his men to shoot in the middle of a caravan made up of their wives and families.

We were closing in on the station, drunk with emotion from the triumph of our collective strength, when I heard a hair-raising shriek. I saw Gabriel in hand-to-hand combat with one of the auto-defensas near the front door. Amparo was trying to break them up, but they were too bound up in the brutal fight. The para was overtaking Mono. His gun was pointed at him, and he was ready to shoot. I knew then that I was going to lose my Gabriel. I grabbed the gun I had hidden in my skirt, pulled it out, and flipped the safety.

I moved in, sidestepping bullets, posters, and soldiers all around me. Gabriel was struggling to breathe as the para choked him with one hand, while the other jammed the barrel of the gun into his neck.

"No more war! No more hate! No more blood!" was echoing in my ears. I felt an astonishing power swirling inside me. One, two, three steps. I was standing right behind the enemy. I didn't think. I just aimed and emptied my .45 Magnum right into his back.

And then time stood still. The man turned, gasping. I could see he was on the threshold of death. He looked straight at me with his hazel eyes, and they were filled with such immense sorrow. Something deep inside me stirred. Those eyes . . . that mouth . . . that grimace of pain. In his dying face I saw the image of Julián.

Then another agonized shriek sounded on the square. I saw my old friend Carmen rushing forward, and with her was a woman who was racked by grief.

The man had collapsed; he was bleeding out. She threw herself over his failing chest with a heart-rending lament. The young man managed to look at her one last time before he died.

Carmen looked at me, horrified. An overpowering feeling washed over me. I looked at Carmen, pleading. She convulsed with sobs as she pulled me into a hug.

"It's Miguel! It's little Miguel, Comandante Miguel, doña Norma's son, your son!"

My eyes went blurry. The earth gave way under my feet, and I don't remember anything else. In the abyss of my unconscious, I heard distant voices calling: "No more war! No more hate! No more blood!"

Angels of Fire
Mariate

will never be acquitted by divine justice for the death of my son. Still, human justice has absolved me.

With Chacho gone, peace returned to the village of San Juan. The villagers went back home. San Juan is part of the Peace Communities Program working with many villages to stop the horrific bloodshed.

The women in my co-op had set a precedent. We started the Eastern Antioquia Coalition of Women for Peace. We have the support of all the neighboring pueblos, and the new mayor of San Juan is one of our strongest supporters. The police chief don Luciano López was elected mayor unanimously when the former mayor fled for fear of retribution for being an informant. The new mayor is excellent, and everyone respects him. Neither the paramilitaries nor the guerrillas have shown their faces around here again.

The day we buried Miguel, I confronted the fate that I can't seem to shake, that hounds me even now. Everyone applauded what they labeled my heroism, but they didn't know the pain gnawing at my gut. There were few parishioners there when I went into the church; Norma de Restrepo was crying beside his coffin. I armed myself with a determination I did not know I had and went over to her. Carmen introduced us. I expected her to be furiously angry with me. But it was the complete opposite. Norma de Restrepo came over to me, took my arm, and said: "You saved the life of the son you knew. One of them had to die; Miguel had been lost to all of us for so long, lost even to himself."

"The mark of Cain," I nodded, as I remembered the words of the Reverend Madre Susana.

"The mark of Cain," Norma repeated, recalling her sister-in-law's admonition.

We left the church together and led the procession behind our son's coffin. Amparo followed the entourage with her family. Miguel's death had served to join the paths of those of us who had marked his life.

From that moment on, Norma and I channeled our shared grief to turn it into redemption. Norma—not doña and not señora—joined the Coalition of Women for Peace as soon as she fully understood that we were both victims of the senselessness of war.

When Gabriel and Rafa found out they were related to the para coman- dante, they finally understood the magnitude of the paradox of their own lives. Now that the ELN is negotiating to hand over its weapons and sign a cease- fire, it's a good time for Gabriel to take advantage of reinsertion and accept his destiny. He hasn't done it yet. He thinks that if he does he will betray an ideal. Maybe the very one I inculcated in him. Rafa changed his name and his appearance so he won't stir up trouble with his old gang. It is not easy for them to leave that way of life and risk the consequences of defection from their respective forces. Both must start to live inside the legal system. This year they registered to finish high school in Medellín. As their adoptive mother, Norma has assumed the tuition and all their expenses. She said it was the least she could do. I could not refuse. How could I? She says that by having an active role in my sons' lives and channeling her energy to a collective cause, she can beat back her depression. They have given her a reason to live.

Amparo is studying journalism at the University of Antioquia in Medellín. She says she wants to be a reporter. She has been so important to Gabriel's efforts to adjust to city life and the challenges of living within the law. When I see them together, full of youth and love, hope springs anew.

Norma, Amparo, and I met at Miguel's tomb in the San Juan cemetery on the second anniversary of his death. We all agreed that our boy's sacrifice would be worth it when everyone involved could let blame go, stop hating, and begin a new path toward living together in peace. On that day an old friend and com- pañera I hadn't seen in a long time reappeared, which made me so very happy.

Norma gave me three ceramic figurines of the three highest archangels in the heavens: Miguel, Gabriel and Rafael. I have them at the head of my bed, and they keep me company no matter where my boys are. I only hope that one day my sons and their descendants will be able to go into life not as agents of death, but as messengers of hope.

Epilogue
Nora

I was assigned the task of attending the Peace Communities Arts and Crafts Fair in Santa Fe de Antioquia, as a delegate of the United Nations Organization for Conflict Resolution.

The tapestry entitled "Mujer" won first prize. It was woven in natural-toned agave strands and featured a woman with her back to us, emerging from the flames of hell, contorted in pain, her arms outstretched to the heavens, trying to touch the clouds where celestial cherubim held out their hands to her. It was signed "M. T. Giraldo." The other pieces all depicted social scenes and themes related to the armed conflict. There was one finalist in the Peace section that caught my eye. It was a banner with the slogan: "No more war! No more hate! No more blood!" It was called "The San Juan Triumph." I wanted to know who the artists were.

"These are from the Eastern Antioquia Peace Community," the coordinator said. She gave me a brochure explaining the movement's origin and mission. There was a newspaper article, too:

"A Caravan of Women Stops Massacre in the San Juan Municipality"—El Colombiano

Medellín, July 20, 2002. Shouting and chanting "No more war," a group of women thwarted a massacre in a guerrilla vs. paramilitary confrontation in the northeastern Antioquia village of San Juan.

The women were armed with posters and unflappable will and burst into the middle of the combat zone carrying flags and chanting: "No more war! No more hate! No more blood!" That was how they stripped the soldiers of the weapons they were pointing at one another.

The women, led by María Teresa Giraldo, created the Eastern Antioquia Peace Community. Its members are mothers, wives, and daughters committed to the cause of ending the war and getting their men back. This is a notable example of how people are rejecting the armed conflict that has been dragging on for more than half a century in this violence-ridden nation.

María Teresa Giraldo? It can't be! Mariate, la sardina? My dear friend, my partner in misadventures? I was so excited as I looked for her among the attendees.

Someone told me that she wasn't there, even though she was one of the winners. She was most likely working at the Peace Community's San Juan offices.

"And where is San Juan?"

I wasted no time, got in my truck and headed out. I soon found that little pueblo hidden in the hills, no thanks to the bad roads or its remote location. I got directions and found the co-op office. But no one was there, either. I asked the owner of the supply shop next to the office if she could tell me where Mariate was. She looked me up and down, suspiciously.

"And who are you?"

"I'm an old friend from years ago. We met in Medellín."

She was inscrutable, so I went on:

"I've been out of the country for years. Look, I was in exile for a long time. I was a revolutionary too, but now I'm working for peace. I'm part of a human rights organization. Have you heard of Amnesty International? Not long ago I came back to Colombia as a U.N. delegate."

I don't know if my words had any effect, but something I said must have struck a chord because finally she introduced herself as doña Celina and told me that doña Tere was at the cemetery. Today was the second anniversary of her son's death.

"Her son? What son?"

She was afraid to give information to a stranger and didn't respond.

I found Mariate at the cemetery, but she wasn't alone. She looked worn, as if centuries were weighing down on her, not just her scant forty years. Her black hair, once so shiny, was now graying. Life had run furrows into her face. There were two women with her. One was older; she tried to hide her sorrow behind a smile of resignation. The other was younger and very pretty, but she already bore the indelible mark of life, too. She was walking between the two, arm-in-arm, linking them. I drew near, and Mariate caught sight of me. She was stunned and ran out immediately to meet me.

"Nora! Amiga! It's been so long!"

We drew each other into a long, warm hug born of so many shared years and experiences. Then she introduced me to her friends.

Norma de Restrepo and Amparo López greeted me with kindness.

"What are you doing here?" I asked.

No one answered. But no one needed to. When I leaned over to look at the name on the tombstone, I understood:

MIGUEL ANGEL RESTREPO ALVAREZ, 1979–2002

What happened next has already been told. We headed to Mariate's, and there, over hot agua de panela and arepa, the three of them tumbled over each other's words as they told me their stories, each from her own point of view. That was when I decided to write this story in three voices. Or is it four?

Perseverance is healing's nurse. It feeds the essential processes of memory, recovery, and renewal in helping us, individually and collectively, to mend, restore, and rebuild. Transcending dreams pushed aside as too difficult to be possible—peace in the homeland—embodies core values through human actions for national healing and rebuilding. Like the portrayals in *Spiral of Silence*, mothers and daughters resolved to protect and nurture their families and communities also strengthen the very backbone of *patria*, which truly makes them heroes. As William Manchester reminded us in *A World Lit Only by Fire* (1992), "deliberate, never mindless . . . the hero acts . . . without encouragement, relying solely on conviction and [her] own inner resources. Shame does not discourage [her]; neither does obloquy."

Since 2000 more than three hundred Colombian women's organizations have arisen in chorus proclaiming no more war, bloodshed, and hatred. Their slogans are these:

"Las mujeres no parimos hijos para la guerra!"
(Women don't have babies for war!)

"Ni un peso ni un paso para la guerra!"
(No *peso*, no step goes toward war!)

"Las mujeres Paz harán!"
(Women will make peace!)

"Ni una guerra que nos mate, ni una paz que nos oprima!"
(No war to kill us, no peace to oppress us!)

These slogans, and others like them, have forged an awareness by standing against the winds of war in a conflict engulfing too many generations.

Peace organizations have united to denounce and oppose armed groups from all political sides: revolutionary groups, paramilitaries, military, and the state. Their actions have generated trust and solidarity from all sectors of civil society. Through their efforts, pivotal actions recognizing rights and compensation for victims of war became legal instances, including the landmark Victims and Land Restitution Law of 2011.

Initiatives by women's groups also atracted attention from international organizations, such as ONU Mujeres, Amnesty International, and Human Rights Watch, providing support and visibility at international level. Lastly, these efforts had a pivotal impact on the peace process held in Havana between the Colombian government and the revolutionary FARC group. These accords were signed in 2016, and marked new beginnings in an unprecedented agreement integrating the voices of the victims, the perpetrators, and the state. Colombia has become a model of bringing to term a challenging process of hope and reconciliation, although even now much healing is yet to be done.

When I wrote *Spiral of Silence* in the first decade of the new millennium, many of these initiatives were just at the seed. I never envisioned that the cry portrayed by the women's cooperative at the end of the novel foresaw the clamor of real women connecting efforts and strength against a war that had lasted so many decades. The prediction has come true, and hopefully, Colombia will finally see the light at the end of the tunnel and will cast off the dubious title of site of Latin America's longest political conflict, in favor of one of inspiration as it ushers in a historical transition to a postconflict era.

Afranio, Parra. 1944–1989. Co-founder of the M-19.

Almarales, Andrés. 1935–1985. Co-founder of the M-19.

Caballerizas. Literally "army stables"; stables near the Batallón Cantón Norte in Usaquén, the military brigade headquarters, where torture sessions were carried out.

Camilo Torres, Father. 1926–1966. Founder of the first sociology program in Latin America, member of the ELN, and fore-grounder of liberation theology.

Canas al aire. Pamphlets written and distributed in the prison. Literally, *canas al aire* means "let your hair down," but taken separately, *cana* is also slang for "prison," and *al aire* can mean "on the air." So the title is playing with all those meanings—letting your hair down in prison with the dissemination of information.

Chiqui. Carmenza Cardona Londoño (1953), member of the M-19, best known for participating in the negotiations to resolve the Dominican Embassy crisis. http://www.eltiempo.com/archivo/documento/MAM-1288357. Accessed April 15, 2013.

Mono Jojoy. Victor Julio Suárez Rojas (1951–2010), also known as Jorge Briceño Suárez, Fuerzas Armadas Revolucionarias de Colombia, FARC, (Revolutionary Armed Forces of Colombia) leader.

El Picotazo. Pamphlets written and distributed in the prison. *Picotazo* references the name of the prison, Picota, but with its own connotations. The suffix "azo" is added to words to emphasize that something is terribly difficult or painful. So *picotazo* (referencing *picadura*) can mean a bee sting or bug bite that is very big and painful; in the context of *Bogotazo*, the suffix emphasizes the violent riots in Bogotá following the 1948 assassination of Jorge Eliécer Gaitán. For *Picotazo*, then, the word emphasizes the hardships of the political prisoners inside La Picota.

Tirofijo. Manuel Marulanda (1930–2008), legendary leader of the Fuerzas Armadas Revolucionarias de Colombia, FARC, (Revolutionary Armed Forces of Colombia). His nickname "Tirofijo" means "Sureshot."

Turco. Literally, "The Turk," nickname for Alvaro Fayad (1946–1986), co-founder of the M-19.

La Violencia. The most violent span of history in Colombia (1948–1958). The decade of violence was sparked by tensions between the Liberal and Conservative parties following the transfer of power to the Conservatives in 1946.

1946	Violence erupts in Colombian countryside between followers of the Conservative Party and the Liberal Party
1948	Assassination of Jorge Eliécer Gaitán, leader of the Liberal Party, in Bogotá, triggering the period known as "La Violencia"
1948–58	La Violencia: Liberal and Conservative armies and guerrillas clash
1951	Liberal peasants organize self-defense groups to fight against the Conservative *pájaros*
1955	General Rojas Pinilla has backing of both parties to lead a coup to oust President Laureano Gómez; Rojas Pinilla is installed as dictator
	Susana, from a Liberal family, falls in love with Alfonso, from a Conservative family; she becomes pregnant
	Susana's Liberal father arranges her illegal, forced abortion
	Susana's and Alfonso's families feud; Susana and Ricardo's house burns down
	Susana and Ricardo flee with their aunt, who arranges for Susana to become a nun and Ricardo to begin military school
1958	Liberal and Conservative parties agree to share power; this is called the National Front and it lasts for 16 years (excluding other parties)
1960s	Camilo Torres, the "revolutionary priest," creates the People's United Front. Several guerrilla groups are formed in this period: the Revolutionary Armed Forces of Colombia (FARC); the National Liberation Army (ELN); the People's Liberation Army (EPL)

1970s	More revolutionary groups appear: the urban guerrilla group the April 19 Movement (M-19); the indigenous group named after Quintín Lame; Worker's Self-Defense (ADO); and the Worker's Revolutionary Party (PRT)
1974	The M-19 steals Simón Bolívar's sword from the Bolivar Museum in Bogotá
1978	*Mariate and Julián meet*
	Norma and Ricardo marry
December 31	M-19 organizes theft of army weapons from the Cantón Norte military base
1979	*Mariate and Julián land in jail*
	Mariate meets Nora
November 9	*Miguel is born*
1980	M-19 takes over the embassy of the Dominican Republic
	Riots in the prisons; *Mariate in solitary confinement*
	Miguel given to Norma and Ricardo Restrepo
1981–82	Muerte a Secuestradores (MAS; Death to Kidnappers) is formed with the support of drug cartels, U.S. corporations, Colombian politicians, and wealthy landowners. While drug traffickers form their paramilitary groups, the military also forms its legal counterinsurgency groups
1982–86	Conservative President Belisario Betancur initiates peace processes with the guerrillas and offers a general amnesty for all armed groups
1982	*Mariate and Julián released through the amnesty*
	Mariate begins search for Miguel
1983	*Gabriel is born*
1985	*Mariate finds Miguel*
	Nora visits Mariate to invite her to join ELN

The political arm of the FARC, the Patriotic Union (UP), is formed (and thousands of its members are subsequently assassinated in the years immediately following). The EPL forms its political arm, the Popular Front

November 6   The M-19 takes over the Palace of Justice in downtown Bogotá

November 7   *Julián dies. Mariate flees to ELN with Gabriel, pregnant with Rafael*

1986   *Rafael is born and surrendered to Mariate's sister*

The peace processes end. Guerrillas retreat to the mountains. Across the nation, paramilitary and counter-insurgency groups massacre union members and civilians accused of supporting the guerrillas

1989   Liberal President Barco Vargas declares war on drugs, increasing repression. Leading drug traffickers are arrested or killed. Pablo Escobar, leader of notorious Medellín Cartel, begins attacks in response to arrests. Liberal party candidate for president Luis Carlos Galán is assassinated

1990   M-19 agrees to a ceasefire and forms a political party, Democratic Alliance M-19. Its leader, Carlos Pizarro, is assassinated during his presidential campaign

1990–94   Liberal César Gaviria's administration begins constitutional reform

1992   Pablo Escobar turns himself in

1993   Pablo Escobar escapes. Escobar's organization recruits adolescent boys and children from Medellín's slums to serve as his hitmen. "Los Pepes," a group of Escobar's victims, joins forces with the army to search for and kill Escobar in December

1995   Paramilitary groups form the Self-Defense Units of Colombia, led by drug kingpin Carlos Castaño. Violence and displacement of civilians increases

Death of Ricardo Restrepo

1996	Women start to organize in local communities to stop the war. Ruta Pacífica de las Mujeres, a national network of women, is born
1998	Conservative President Andrés Pastrana explores peace talks with FARC. Creates demilitarized zone during negotiations
1999	Formal peace talks begin with FARC
2000	United States grants Colombia nearly $1 billion to fight drug trafficking and rebels, through Plan Colombia
	Mariate retires from ELN and moves to San Juan. She forms the co-op as doña Tere
2001	Iniciativa de Mujeres por la Paz (Women for Peace Initiative) formed, a network of women's organizations working to implement an agenda within peace negotiation processes
	National March for Peace organized by women; more than 400,000 people march for peace and reconciliation
2002	Peace process with FARC broken
	Independent Alvaro Uribe becomes president, promises to eliminate rebels
	Amparo meets Chacho. Amparo meets Mono
July	*Death of don Eusebio. The village of San Juan shuts down*
	Death of Madre Susana after she reveals she has Miguel's birth certificate
	Chacho and his men take San Juan
	Norma seeks Mariate with Carmen and is held hostage by guerrillas
	Amparo seeks Chacho to save San Juan, and is held by Chacho and his group
	Mariate (doña Tere) uses co-op to organize for peace
July 19	*Miguel dies by the hand of his mother*

2003	United Self-Defense Force (AUC) begins to disarm
2004	AUC begins peace talks with government

Iniciativa de Mujeres por la Paz and Ruta Pacífica de las Mujeres hold the first National Meeting of Women against War. Their slogan: "No war to kill us, no peace to oppress us"

Nora and Mariate reunite at Miguel's grave